a PORTHKENNACK
CONTEMPORARY

BROKE DEEP

CHARLIE COCHRANE

RIPTIDE
PUBLISHING

Riptide Publishing
PO Box 1537
Burnsville, NC 28714
www.riptidepublishing.com

Broke Deep
Copyright © 2017 by Charlie Cochrane

Cover art: G. D. Leigh, blackjazzdesign.com
Editors: Sarah Lyons, Carole-ann Galloway
Layout: L.C. Chase, lcchase.com/design.htm

ISBN: 978-1-62649-543-2

First edition
June, 2017

Also available in ebook:
ISBN: 978-1-62649-542-5

a PORTHKENNACK
CONTEMPORARY

BROKE DEEP

CHARLIE COCHRANE

RIPTIDE
PUBLISHING

To the wooden walls of England and those who risked their lives sailing in them.

TABLE OF
CONTENTS

CHAPTER
ONE

Morgan turned the letter in his hands. Pointless bloody exercise, really; whichever way up it was, the thing would read the same.

"It isn't you, Morgan, it's me."

Trust James to have ended things with a cliché. Maybe he'd typed *Dear John letters* into Google, cut and pasted what he'd found, changed the name John for the name Morgan and copied out the resulting text longhand.

"It's been great, all of it, but people change. We've grown, and not in the same direction."

The James he'd spent so long with wouldn't have been able to create such eloquent prose, not without his secretary taking his rough notes to make them into something impressive, as she'd done for him in the past. Please God she hadn't been allowed anywhere near this.

A simple, *I'm bored with you so I'm buggering off*, would have been more in James's line. Or, *You're no longer the spring chicken who caught my eye. I couldn't be seen going out with a bloke about to hit thirty. Not good for the image.*

Morgan had always suspected James kept half an eye on whether there was anything better about. Like a pet cat, seemingly devoted to its owner, but ready to push off and relocate if he found a better household. Morgan's family had once had a moggy like that; he hadn't thought he'd end up with a boyfriend who'd show the same proclivities.

"I won't insult you by asking if we can remain friends, although I hope someday we can be civil enough to share a pint. For old times' sake."

So that he could tell Morgan about his latest bloke? Like he used to talk about Jonny and say he'd only been a practice run for the real thing? Morgan slapped the letter on the table. He wasn't ready to be civil. Especially after three years of James hinting that the real thing might be *him*. That had been a load of crap, hadn't it? Like all the other crap James had been spouting these last few months. Why had it taken Morgan so long to realise he'd been strung along?

It wasn't like he hadn't been expecting the letter, or something like it, but those cold, hard words still hurt like a kick in the guts. All right, it was better than being dumped by text message—or over Facebook, that treacherous change in status from *in a relationship* to *single*—but only just. Why couldn't the bastard have had the guts to drive down to Cornwall and tell him face-to-face?

Because, truth be told, James was a coward, a man who'd do anything to avoid a scene or put off a confrontation. Getting somebody else to travel down and deliver the bad news would have suited his style, if he could have got away with it.

Morgan screwed the letter up, flung it into the dustbin, and resolved never to think of James Price again. Or at least not for the next ten minutes.

That was all the time it took to make a decent, mud-strong mug of tea and take it out to the garden. If he could survive the next ten minutes without thinking of James the bastard, then he could survive another ten and then another. Like giving up smoking, one cigarette at a time. What he needed was distraction, either general or particular. At least his garden still brought him the happiness that had been sorely absent from his life the last year. He sat on his favourite wooden bench, took a deep breath and half closed his eyes.

Late April was turning out lovely, an early burst of summer in full swing, and the garden of Cadoc, his house, formed the sort of sun trap which became almost unbearable on a hot August day but which proved perfect when spring or autumn turned kind. Morgan listened to the bees, watched the trees and the flowers, and tried not to think of all the times in the past he'd sat here with James.

Count your blessings right now before you go mad.

Blessing one, living in London, the thick air and continual noise, was behind him. Blessing two, working from home and being able to nip out here for the perfect way of clearing his mind, letting his stress dissolve away into the calm sea air.

Only, at the moment, Morgan would have been pleased to be head down in a noisy office, with sights and sounds and externally imposed deadlines to take his mind off that bloody letter and the fact that his life seemed to be falling apart piece by piece. He swatted at a late-flowering tulip with his foot, cursing it for sticking its handsome head up and mocking him with its *joie de vivre*.

Sod tulips, sod the sunshine and sod James Price.

Morgan swigged back his tea. Right. Life was going to go on, irrespective of how many flowers he kicked the heads off, and if he sat down and thought about things objectively, it might go on a lot more enjoyably without James. In the long run. One day he'd look back at this event as being constructive, despite it hurting like stink now.

Why not count the points in favour of a clean break? Surely there had to be some?

James was a control freak—if things weren't going as *he* wanted them to, then they were wrong. His sense of humour had changed, so he only seemed to enjoy jokes at other people's expense. Morgan had always managed to ignore the roving eye, pretending it was nothing different to admiring the delicacies on the Waitrose cake counter. It didn't mean you were going to indulge, did it? Except that James had quite possibly been sampling every cake in the box on the sly. It would have been typical of the bastard, and he'd have covered his tracks in the process.

We never did have any realistic future, did we?

Morgan blew out his cheeks—wasn't this process supposed to be making him feel better? The voice in his head was right, though. Even if they'd got as far as tying the knot, James might have managed to find a dozen ways to slip through it. And that wasn't what Morgan had wanted, no matter how he'd tried to persuade himself that *he'd* be the one to make a difference, the Mr. Right who'd keep James on the straight and narrow.

Reason said that he should be pleased to have got the letter, to be shot of James and shot of uncertainty all at once. But all his objective reasoning couldn't logic away such a ball of pain in his stomach.

The sudden, insistent bleating of the telephone started Morgan out of his remembrances of times past, pleasant and obnoxious. It would be a client, probably, wanting a quote over the phone for a particularly intricate design contract. That would be a good distraction. Not that he was short of work—there was plenty to tide him over—but some kind of project to really stretch his brains would keep his mind off painful things.

"Cadoc Design. Hello?" Morgan's practiced tones managed to sound both welcoming and businesslike, or so he'd been informed when it had been a friend rather than a client at the other end of the line.

"Oh, sorry. Think I've got the wrong number."

"Not to worry, it's—" Morgan didn't have the chance to finish, the abrupt tones of the dialling code signalling that the phone at the other end had been put down. Wrong number? He couldn't remember the last one of those he'd had, not since the time he'd been plagued with calls to his mobile by someone who'd been convinced he was a pizza delivery service. Not worth ringing 1471 if it was a genuine mistake. He'd got as far as the kitchen, looking to wrest another mug of tea out of the pot, when the phone went again, and he turned on his heels to answer it again.

"Cadoc Design. *Hello?*" He felt less friendly this time.

"Sorry, it's me again." That was obvious from the same dithering voice. "I definitely haven't misdialled, so either I've been given the wrong number in the first place or you're Morgan Capell."

"You haven't and I am." He'd ditched the polite edge completely. Who could be ringing him out of the blue and what did he want if he wasn't a customer? If the idiot was trying to sell Morgan his wares, all he'd get was an earful of abuse; cold calls were the bane of everyone's life, and on a day like today, he had no patience left.

"Right. Sorry to be so useless. I'm dreadful on the phone."

He could say that again. At least whoever this was came across too awkwardly to be a salesman—no suggestion of smooth talking, and too long a pause in the conversation. Morgan took a deep breath. "I have no idea who you are, but I assume there's something you want to talk about that isn't to do with web design?"

"Yes. The wreck of the *Troilus.*"

"Oh." Morgan felt his tongue tie itself in knots, as it always did when that particular ship got mentioned. What did this guy want to know about her? And how could he both have got Morgan's number and known Morgan would have a tale to tell?

"I suppose you want to know how I got hold of you?" The voice on the phone sounded more apologetic than ever. Telepathic, with it.

"That might be a good place to start."

"Your friend James gave me it."

"Oh." Double *oh* with fucking knobs on. So, not only had James the bastard left him high and dry, he was giving people Morgan's number at random so they could ring about matters intensely personal? How many years would Morgan get for wringing his ex-boyfriend's neck, and would they be worth it? "What did he tell you?"

"Only that the ship went down near where you live. I'm trying to research the history of her midshipmen, the ones who got transferred elsewhere before she sank and the unlucky ones who went on the rocks with her." The voice was gaining in confidence, clearly on a pet subject. "Sorry, I should have introduced myself. Dominic. Dominic Watson."

Morgan wasn't sure what to say next, as the introduction the other way had already been done and without his consent. "What is it you want to know? I can't tell you anything about the ship's officers." The prickles of unease that had appeared on Morgan's neck wouldn't go away. The *Troilus*. He hadn't thought of her in weeks.

"I wasn't expecting that you could." Dominic sounded as if he was used to being unlucky. "My request's a bit different. James said that you've got several of the ship's timbers in your house?"

"Yes, that's right. The locals made the most of what they could find washed up—there was enough to put some roof timbers in here." Impressive ones, too. You could still see the stepping of the mast in one place, but Morgan wasn't going to mention that at the moment. Wouldn't do to get this Dominic bloke too excited and have him threatening to get straight in the car, camera in hand. There were other reasons, as well, why Morgan didn't want to raise the issue of this particular ship and not even James had been aware of all of them.

"Wow." Dominic seemed really impressed, nonetheless. "I tried to find some pictures on the internet, but all I get is the old engraving of the wreck and a diagram of the ship's lines. Nothing about your house."

"That would be right. I've never posted any pictures of the beams, and my parents wouldn't have dreamed of anything like that." They'd been highly protective of their little bit of history, when Dad had still been alive and Mum had been compos mentis enough to care. They'd have hated to end up as part of the tourist trail. "It's a private property. I don't give guided tours."

"Oh."

"Sorry, I didn't mean to be so rude." That last remark had been a step too far; the thought of his mother when she'd been well had brought the old anger to the surface. Dear God, it had been over a year since she went into the nursing home—was he never going to get used to it? "I just want to be sure you're doing a proper study and not indulging in a *Hornblower* fandom fest."

"Mr. Capell, I can assure you that I'm involved in family research." Dominic's voice sounded cold and suddenly very clipped. "Our history is connected to that ship, and there have been too many half-truths told that I'd like to put straight."

Morgan swallowed hard, guilt making him inclined to generosity. "My apologies. Look, I think we've got off on the wrong foot here. Your call caught me unawares. I'm not used to people wanting to come and gawp at the cottage."

"No, you don't need to apologise. I shouldn't have barged in like that. James told me that it wasn't a well-known thing about the beams and that the family were rather protective of their architectural inheritance." Dominic sighed. "Maybe he didn't realise how serious I am about the subject."

"He was probably showing off." That was James to a tee. Morgan wondered whether Dominic was gay and any (or all) of young, handsome, and available. It would explain why the rat had suddenly decided to start revealing Cadoc's secrets. "Write me a letter, Mr. Watson."

"Excuse me?"

"If you're serious, write me a letter. Explain exactly what you're researching and what you'd hope to gain by coming to see the timbers." Morgan felt empowered, as though this would somehow help get revenge on James for his blabbing. "I can't stop you coming down here and visiting the wreck site—anyone can take the path to Gull Point to get a view of the Devil's Anvil—but if you want to get in here, you'll have to persuade me."

"You're on." Dominic chuckled, maybe at the geography lesson, because anyone could find out about the cliff path by consulting a decent local map, especially somebody so avid. "Can you give me your full address?"

"No. That can be your first job. You've got *my* name and phone number and anything else James handed over. Get on the internet and find out the rest. If that defeats you, then you're no bloody use as a researcher." Morgan grinned.

"Actually, he didn't give me anything else. Name of your house, road, nothing." Dominic didn't sound too perturbed. "But I'll take up the challenge. That letter will be with you by the end of the week. Thanks."

"No problem—" The click at the end of the line cut off Morgan midsentence. He considered the empty mug in his hand—he'd never got that top up—and shook his head. What the hell had all that been about? And what was he going to do if a letter actually came?

A letter arrived two days later, an elegant white envelope clattering through the letterbox alongside a charity catalogue, a bill, and an advert from the bank.

Mr. M Capell
Cadoc
Headland Road
Porthkennack
PL28 7RY

The postcode wasn't quite right, but it was close enough, although the postmark was so smudged it could have come from Outer Mongolia. Probably a circular, although it was unusual to get a handwritten one, and who the hell was writing to him with what appeared to be a genuine fountain pen?

James had always complained about Morgan's habit of leaving the most interesting letters until last and making a song and dance about trying to work out who had sent them. *He'd* have ripped the thing open and put everyone out of their misery.

You bloody idiot. How could Morgan be so dumb? This had to be from . . . what was his name? Derek? Dominic? Dominic.

The memory stopped him in his tracks, all inclination to open the thing suddenly gone. Morgan had never supposed the bloke was going to follow up his interest in the wreck of the *Troilus*. He debated screwing up the whole lot, letter and envelope and all, sticking it in the bin, and forgetting about it, but that wasn't really an option anymore, was it? He'd asked Dominic to do the research and since Dominic had come up with the goods, then *he* had to do his part of the bargain and at least give him a chance.

He looked at the address again, wondering how easy it had been to find him. Maybe Dominic had bypassed the research stage and gone straight to James? Morgan hoped that wasn't the case; the sooner he could get any vestige of that miserable bastard out of his life, the better. Probably the fact he'd answered that original phone call with the name of his business had made the challenge too easy.

He bit the bullet, took out the letter, and read.

Dear Mr. Capell,

I'm assuming my search for an address has led me to the right place, although you never can be sure with the internet. If it hasn't, and some kind soul hasn't realised my mistake and passed this on, I suppose you'll never know.

Despite the sick feeling in his stomach, Morgan grinned. Dominic seemed to have fallen straight out of a BBC sitcom, with his self-deprecation, apologetic tone, and unusual turn of phrase. Morgan put the letter down and poured a coffee; if this was a torture to be endured, then it should be as comfortable a torture as possible.

I studied history at Durham and now, for my sins, I've converted to accountancy. A sensible career choice for someone who wants to have plenty of resources, not the least of them time, to pursue his hobby. By which I mean nautical research, specifically related to my family. I'm not certain how to convince you of my authenticity on that point, as I've yet to have anything published, although I enclose a copy (of a copy!) of part of Troilus's *muster from 1793, the year before she sank. This is the nearest to "papers" I can produce.*

This time Morgan laughed aloud. Surely Dominic wasn't this formal in person? Rather than the ripped bloke he'd visualised James trying to impress, he now pictured a bespectacled, bookish guy in clothes that had gone out of fashion ten years previously, waving his hands about as he spoke.

I hope that you'll treat my request seriously. I don't want to come and gawp at your house, like a photographer for the tabloids. My intention would simply be to take photos of the beams. (Do they have any carpenters' marks like the ones at Chesapeake Mill? In that case I'd like to take the equivalent of a brass rubbing, if that's convenient.)

However unpleasant this might prove, Morgan felt duty bound to invite Dominic over. Had his mum still been well enough to advise him, she'd have insisted there were no reasonable grounds for refusal. He resumed reading.

I'll be investigating the Porthkennack area, obviously; I believe there are some sailors' graves in a local churchyard. It seems the locals did better than the inhabitants of the Scilly Isles did by Cloudesley Shovell. Still, I suppose the Cornish have always been on the respectable side.

Morgan snorted with laughter. *Respectable?* Dominic must have had his tongue stuffed well and truly in his cheek. Why not indulge him? Why not have a "be kind to a nerd day"?

"You never used to be so cruel." His mother's remembered voice resounded in his mind with one of the last things she'd said to him before she'd moved into the home. *"Not before you took up with James."*

And she'd been right, although he'd not admitted that until now; he used to be a better man than this. He returned to the letter with a kinder eye. *I'd like to take pictures of the surrounding area; if you have any specialised knowledge of the local wrecks, or could refer me to anyone who does, I'd be extremely grateful. There is a family connection to all this, as I said, but I'd rather explain that face-to-face.*

Now, have I passed your test? If the answer is yes, please write to me at the address given above. If not, I shall still visit the area, but I promise not to come and make a nuisance of myself.

Yours sincerely,
Dominic Watson

Morgan had to read the letter again, for amusement. Even if Dominic hadn't satisfied him with his obviously genuine enthusiasm for his subject, the communication in itself would have won him over. It was like slipping into a time warp and finding yourself getting a letter from somebody straight out of P.G. Wodehouse. *Mind you, that's what James used to say about me. He probably meant it as a compliment at first, but the appeal soon died.*

Maybe Dominic would appreciate that part of Morgan's character; it was as good a reason as any for meeting him.

What if it means thinking about the Troilus *again? You should put yourself first. You know what the thought of that wreck does to you.*

Unease crept up his spine like an icy hand as he reread the letter, Dominic's enthusiasm for the wreck shining through, but Morgan couldn't spend his entire life avoiding the subject. If it wasn't Dominic, it would be someone else talking about *Troilus*; Morgan had to deal with it. He got nightmares about the ship going down, that was all.

All? Since the first time he'd had the dream as a teenager, it had come back with startling regularity, like an old film that's never off the television. To talk to Dominic about the shipwreck was to risk the dream returning when he'd kept it at bay for so long, but he had no choice now; the gauntlet he'd thrown down had been picked up again pretty speedily. He'd invite him down for the first May bank holiday weekend, as that would at least give them both a few days to prepare. He couldn't believe he'd be lucky enough to find that Dominic would already have plans and they'd have to push the date back further.

Dominic not having provided a phone number, Morgan posted a reply the next day, afraid that if he delayed too long, he'd be tempted to rip the bloody letter up and simply hope that Dominic and his research went away. Ingrained values wouldn't let him be so gung-ho—his mother would have killed him for such rudeness, back in the days when things like proper manners still mattered to her. He had to reply and expect a prompt response, given that Dominic, despite his slightly odd and old-fashioned style, seemed pretty determined.

For all Morgan's perceptiveness about Dominic's resolve, the swiftness of the bloke's reply hitting the front door mat at Cadoc still surprised him. There had to have been an unprecedented juxtaposition of vans and trains and postmen to have turned the correspondence around so quickly.

Morgan didn't dilly-dally about opening the envelope this time, nor did he need a crystal ball to predict that the answer would be a resounding *Yes, please.*

He'd been right about having to face things sooner rather than later. No matter how much he tried to slip out of *Troilus's* grasp, she seemed determined to pin him down.

CHAPTER TWO

The first Saturday in May brought a mellowing of the weather. May Day weekend had obviously decided to put on a show, with sunshine predicted as far as the BBC's weather forecasters dared to go and, for once, it appeared they'd got it right. Morgan had spent a few hours in the garden on Friday evening, tidying up the last of the spring flowers in the semi-wild border and encouraging the early bedding to get itself established.

Saturday morning, Morgan decided to tidy the house. He might only be having Dominic as his guest once, but Mum would have insisted Dominic see Cadoc at its best. The beams got a thorough going over with a feather duster, surprising some of the spiders which had taken up residence, and the whole place—never really that dirty or untidy—shone like a new pin. It was good to have something, or somebody, to spruce the house up for; it had been too long since Morgan had done any entertaining.

When Morgan had his music on loud, the doorbell tended to be drowned out, so he'd resisted any temptation to have the hi-fi on this morning. He'd given Dominic clear directions to the house, Cadoc being tucked away at the end of a little Cornish lane, parts of which appeared to be almost impassable to the untrained eye. The scan of the map which he'd tucked in the envelope would prove more reliable to Dominic than anything he could download from Google.

He couldn't help feeling sorry for the bloke. Poor, fanatical thing, getting excited over half a dozen lumps of wood.

You're doing it again.

Catching himself thinking as James might have thought sparked off a bout of guilt which, in turn, produced a resolution to make his guest a pot of really good coffee. He'd also planned a lunch of soup, sandwiches, and a plate of Waitrose biscuits, from when he'd stocked up.

Late morning, the doorbell went off with its horribly insistent tone. Morgan smoothed his hair and put on a smile—the best smile he could manage on a day when he'd woken at five o'clock in the morning and not managed to get back to sleep. The fact his waking had interrupted an erotic dream involving James hadn't made things any easier.

He was bloody glad he'd made some effort on his appearance when he glimpsed the vision of hotness through the hall window. This had to be a lost surfer boy or someone who'd come to the coast to find himself a job as a lifeguard and got hopelessly off track. It couldn't be Dominic, because blokes like this didn't usually knock on the door of Cadoc for any legitimate reason.

Morgan hesitated, hand on the doorknob. If real life was like a gay romance book, this *would* be Dominic and they'd bond over a discussion of James, one full of shared hatred for the bloke. The next minute they'd be taking a romantic walk on the beach, and maybe tonight they'd drag each other up the stairs and . . .

The doorbell rang again, and Morgan realised he was still standing fantasising. He opened the door in a rush just as "surfer boy who might be Dominic" had turned to go back down the path.

"Sorry I took so long," Morgan said, as brightly as he could manage.

"I thought there was nobody in." Surfer Boy smiled, which reignited memories of last night's dream. Morgan squirmed. "There's a guy here to see you, only he's gone off to take some pictures, and he asked me to come over and say he'd arrived." Surfer Boy waved airily at a bright-red hire car, parked next to the gate.

"Are you a friend of his?" Surely this couldn't be Dominic's boyfriend, although his twin brother would be a good outcome.

"No. We met on the plane, and when he heard where I was heading, he said he'd give me a lift so I didn't have to wait for a bus. My girlfriend lives up on the main road." Surfer Boy grinned, looking stupidly handsome, more so for being unavailable. "Stroke of luck on my part. Eh?"

"It worked out well." Morgan sighed as he scanned the line of the hedge. "Has your chauffeur gone walkabout?"

"Probably. He seems a bit of a fanatic; he's got a bee in his bonnet about ships or timbers or whatever. I wasn't paying a lot of attention. I bet he's seen an interesting piece of wood and gone to take a sample or whatever." Surfer Boy—straight, unavailable surfer boy—smiled again, then adjusted his backpack. "Right. Unless I want a dose of earache, I'd better be on my way. Bye." He turned on his heels and walked off down the path towards the gate, duty done.

"Bye," Morgan answered, watching him go and wondering why life was *never* like gay romance books.

There was still no sign of the elusive Dominic. Maybe he'd fallen down a rabbit hole or over the cliff? Morgan stood on the doorstep contemplating this for a good minute before he twigged it was a real, and not very amusing, possibility. People did go arse over tip at the end of the lane, unless they realised in time that they needed to slow down and make a sharp left to carry on along the coastal path, which had been meandering inland. And if the terrain was slippery with mud or they went too far arse over tip, then they'd end up right by the cliff edge, if not over it.

Morgan didn't quite break into a run, but he made it through his garden, out of the gate, and into the road at a lick. He didn't want to seem to be in a panic, especially if he ran into his guest a short stretch down the lane; there was a limit to how much of a plonker even *he* was prepared to appear. There was no sight of the bloke anywhere this side of the cliff path, and no sound of him either. Morgan picked up his pace, although he didn't call out. It wasn't simply a case of saving face—if Dominic, or anyone else come to that, was too near the edge, the shock of a sudden noise could be enough to make them start.

He'd reached the end of the lane, where the hedges stopped and the path turned through its sharp angle, when he saw a lanky figure, camera in hand but not to eye, peering out over the sea. If this was Dominic, at least he had the sense not to position himself right at the edge, especially as he looked like a hefty gust of wind might well blow him off his feet. Quite a contrast to the surfer boy he'd sent to pass on his message.

"Dominic Watson?" Morgan waved, then came closer, appraising his guest with every step, and trying to hide his disappointment.

"That's me. You must be Morgan." Dominic held out his hand. "I'm sorry I didn't come directly to the house. I wanted to see *the* place."

"No problem. I got your message." Morgan resisted all temptation to say *and I approve of your choice of messenger*. He knew nothing about Dominic apart from the enthusiasm for ships. It could be the bloke was rabidly homophobic, his meeting with James notwithstanding—the rat sometimes talked to straight blokes, and not just about business, especially if he thought he had a chance of temporarily converting them.

"That would be Tim. Note I didn't add 'nice but dim,' although I admit I thought it." Dominic grinned. "I met him on the plane from Gatwick. Lovely lad, but hardly the sharpest pencil in the box. I'm glad he managed to find the right house."

"I'll take your word for his mental faculties." He wouldn't mention his appearance. Morgan smiled, staring out towards the Devil's Anvil, although he didn't mention the rocks, either. Nor the wreck. The Anvil wore its harmless face now, barely other than a gentle hog's back of stone breaking the waves. Come low tide, the needles of rock—widow-makers, each one of them—wouldn't be quite so inviting. No wonder they'd stationed the local lifeboat nearby. "We've laid on lovely weather for you, anyway. It was thick with fog yesterday. It said on the radio that they'd had to shut the airport."

"So I heard. I've been keeping an eye on the website, was worried sick I wouldn't be able to get here. Even thought about tackling the A303 and driving down with all the world and his wife and kids." Dominic grimaced. "Glad I didn't have to. Nobody wants to risk getting stuck in a twenty-mile tailback over Salisbury Plain. Still, that would be better than if you lived on Jersey and they shut the airport. Then I'd have to take a boat."

"You're not a good sailor?"

"You can say that again. I feel sick on the Thames." Dominic's grimace turned to a grin. "Come to think of it, I feel sick on the boating lake at the park."

Morgan studied him, sideways on. Now he'd got the image of Tim out of his mind and overcome his initial disappointment, it was clear he'd done Dominic a disservice. He must have been the right side of thirty, and wasn't a bad-looking bloke, in a "tenth Doctor Who" sort of way. Built for speed rather than comfort, all angular edges. It wouldn't be too much of a burden to entertain him for an hour or two. "So what makes you so keen on ships if you can't bear travelling on them?"

Dominic gestured vaguely out to sea. "Haven't you read any of the Hornblower stories? He was sick at Spithead but it didn't stop him becoming an admiral."

"I have read them. Some, anyway. And seeing as you don't seem to be in the navy, then you've not really answered my question."

"Guilty as charged." Dominic made a naval salute. "I have to get my nautical thrills secondhand. I've always been fascinated with the Age of Sail, from the day my parents took me to see *Victory*. I fell in love with her."

They both gazed out over the sea again, where a pleasure boat had rounded the tip of the headland, speeding off in search of dolphins or puffins or some other wildlife to observe; despite its smooth, elegant contours, it couldn't compare to a ship of the line. Perhaps in Dominic's mind's eye he'd a vision of masts and sails and running out the great guns.

"I soon discovered I'd never be able to handle anything more maritime than a sand yacht, so I had to immerse myself in the history. The real-life stories." He turned back, eyes ablaze with enthusiasm. "Occasionally I hope I'll wake up one morning and find myself transported off somewhere through space and time."

Morgan took a deep breath. "Sounds like Doctor Who and his TARDIS," he replied, wishing he could be brave enough to say, *you wouldn't want that in reality, believe me.*

"A TARDIS would be fine so long as I could opt out of meeting the Daleks. They scare me stiff. And I don't want to discover other worlds. There's enough here to keep me happy."

"I suppose landing up in the middies' mess on the *Victory* would feel like being on Mars." Morgan grinned. Dominic was exactly what he'd expected: priceless. "And if you did fetch up there, wouldn't you be plastering it with the contents of your stomach?"

"Probably. But in my imagination I don't have seasickness— that's the beauty of daydreams. Right." Dominic rubbed his hands together. "Would it be rude of me to ask if I can come and see those roof beams while the light's still as good as this?"

"Not rude at all. Isn't that exactly what you came here for?" Morgan pointed towards the house. "Come on. I've got a bite of lunch ready for us."

"It gets better and better." Dominic slipped into step alongside Morgan. "I've not had anything since an early breakfast. Too excited. What my mother used to call butterflies in the stomach."

"I hope they've fluttered off enough for you to get your chops around some soup and sandwiches. There's coffee going too." Tim the surfer boy might have been offered a slab of chocolate cake. Among other things, if he'd been inclined and this had been that bloody romance book.

"There's always room for soup and sandwiches. Is it homemade? The soup, I mean?" Dominic smiled. He had a pleasant, lopsided smile that transformed his everyday type of face into something downright handsome. If Morgan could think of enough things to keep the bloke smiling, then the next few hours could be enjoyable.

"I'm afraid it isn't. Waitrose fresh packed, so at least it's not from a tin." Morgan opened the gate to his garden. "I did make the sandwiches myself. Here, come and see this. It's supposed to be from the wreck—part of the ballast." Funny how he'd almost forgotten about the ballast stone, although he passed by it almost every day. It was part of the wallpaper for him now, too familiar for special notice.

They positioned themselves either side of a large boulder that might once have been a bit of carved Bath stone or similar material.

"Blimey. Where was it found?" Dominic walked around the stone, then knelt down to explore it, tracing his fingers along each line and crevice.

"On the beach, about a week after the ship was lost, or so the family story goes, after an even fiercer storm than the one which took her down. It was found by my no-idea-how-many-greats-grandfather." Morgan nodded. "You can take pictures of it, if you want, but I can't vouch one hundred percent for its provenance. For all I know it was simply a case of my grandmother making up things to entertain us. She told a cracking story."

"'Us'?" Dominic had his camera out and was taking a stream of snaps, from every angle, in full sunlight and in the meagre shade of his own figure.

"My brother Eddie and I, when we were boys."

"Does he still live here?"

"Good God, no. Porthkennack's far too small and provincial for him. He's in the City, making a mint." Morgan shuddered—the prickling resentment he felt over Eddie must be coming over good and strong.

"He's mad, then." Dominic stood up, putting away his camera and scanning the view. "I'd give my eyeteeth to live here; big improvement on Surrey. Would have done since I was a child and arsed around with a net in the rock pools. We came and stayed along this coast every year."

"Is that where your particular interest in *Troilus* comes from? Running across the story of the ship when on holiday?" Things were starting to make sense. Morgan could imagine this strange young man as a strange little boy, poking about in the tourist shops, finding one of the many slim, self-published books aimed at the visiting trade. Sitting in his deckchair reading, fascinated, about the wrecks Cornwall had seen. The thought of a serious young Dominic poring through texts in the local library was oddly endearing.

"In a way. I can't deny it's important she's connected to a place I've always loved." Dominic sighed. "I didn't know about the ship when I holidayed here, though. I wish I had—I could have found out further information about her. But when I started to research the wreck, facts about this particular ship rang a bell. I played on that beach down in the cove." He grinned. "It was always a treat—my parents said it was *our* special place."

"Lots of people stumble across that beach and think it's their own."

"I can imagine. Like stumbling across a piece of paradise. We always had it to ourselves, though."

"That's the benefit of a steep path. It stops all but the hardiest tourists. Come on, you need to see the beams." They headed through the garden.

"I love these old houses." Dominic looked up with clear envy at the gabled windows. "Have you always lived here?"

"Pretty well all my life except when I was at university and just after. Intend to stay here too." Despite the sunshine, Morgan felt suddenly cold. That was what his mother had always hoped, that she'd live to a ripe old age in the house she'd come to as a bride; nowhere in the plan had there been room for seeing out her days in a nursing home. He quickened his pace, until they reached the front door.

"Then you're a lucky man." Dominic hovered, despite Morgan having opened the door and waved him inside. "Shoes off?"

"I'm sorry?"

"Do you want me to take my shoes off? So many people these days don't want their carpets trodden on."

"Blimey, no." Morgan ran his hands through his hair. "Really? How bloody rude."

"That's what I think. Okay if it's part of your culture, but I hate it when possessions take precedence over people." Still, Dominic carefully wiped his shoes on the doormat. He glanced around the hallway. "It's exactly how I imagined it would be from the outside. We used to rent a house similar to this when we were on holiday. There were half a dozen of us by the time Aunty Mary dragged her brood along, so we needed all the space we could get."

There was probably a story to be told about that, given the exasperation in Dominic's voice at the mention of Aunty Mary, but they wouldn't go there now. Maybe if Dominic was staying in the area for a few days, they could meet up over a pint and talk about old times. And was that the lingering influence of Tim the surfer boy, getting Morgan's hormones going?

"Come and see the beams," he said, eager to get his head straight. "I was going to call them the 'famous' beams, only we've managed to keep them out of public view." He opened the door to the kitchen. "They're all through the lower part of the house. It's not so usual to have them still exposed in these type of properties, but they're an object for family pride."

"As they should be. And how you've managed to keep stuff about them off the internet beats me. If I hadn't run into James and the conversation turned in the right direction, I'd have been none the wiser." Dominic got out his camera. "Is it all right to take pictures in the house as well? I'll avoid getting anything in shot that might give away where we are."

"That's fine. The carpenter's marks are clearer in the dining room, but the mast stepping in here is amazing." Morgan pointed towards the top corner of the kitchen, to the left of the old fireplace.

"Fantastic." Dominic beamed. "Bloody fantastic." He started lining up his shots, much more carefully than he'd done with the boulder.

Morgan watched him. The enthusiasm was touching; Dominic clearly loved his hobby, with a schoolboy glee that could have come straight out of a nineteen sixties edition of *The Beano*.

Did he ping the gaydar? That depended on whether you had reliable gaydar to start with. A particularly embarrassing incident in a bar in Plymouth flashed into Morgan's mind, one which had taught him not to leap to conclusions. Some women went mad for camp, and some guys would turn it on to impress *them*.

"I'll get the soup on while you're busy. The dining room's through the hall. Make yourself completely at home."

"Thank you. I'll shout if I get lost or anything." Dominic smiled and headed out the door, unlikely to go too far astray given how straightforward the layout of the house was. Morgan busied himself with the lunch, laying out crockery and cutlery on the breakfast bar. The dining room was out of bounds for eating, and not just because it presently was full of an enthusiastic Age of Sail fan with a roving camera. For as long as Morgan could remember, that room had been reserved for special occasions, big family Christmases, or intimate dinners à deux. He wasn't sure he'd be seeing much of the latter anytime soon and the former had probably gone entirely by the board.

He glanced up from the stove at the picture hanging next to it. Him, James, Mum, and Dad—plus assorted relatives, including Eddie and his obnoxious girlfriend—the last time Christmas lunch had been served on the long dining table. Everyone seemed happy, even James, who wasn't putting on a show for once. They'd all rubbed along together pleasantly enough, behaving themselves under Mum's watchful eye.

He was going to have to find a different picture to replace it, one that didn't remind him of boyfriends past, one that didn't speak so relentlessly of happy times that were never to be recaptured. They'd had some fun back then, him and James. They'd shared a room with Eddie, more like schoolboys than men, sneaking beer and snacks upstairs and sharing blue jokes. Even James, who usually scoffed at such immature things, had seemed to enjoy himself.

There'd been no chance of hanky-panky—if the Capells turned a blind eye to whatever went on away from the roost, there'd be none of it going on under their roof.

"All done. Thanks." Dominic's voice shook Morgan out of his dream. How long had he been standing there, lost in remembrance of things past? Enough time for the soup to have started sticking on the bottom of the pan, anyway.

"My pleasure. Only I'm not sure this soup will be yours." Morgan whipped the pan off the stove before cautiously stirring the contents. "No, might be okay, after all. Perhaps we'd better eat it before I can ruin it further."

He poured the soup into the bowls, then fetched the plate of sandwiches from the fridge.

"Feast fit for a king," Dominic said, looking at the food with evident delight and not the slightest hint of sarcasm. "That'll see me right through to dinnertime."

Morgan grinned. "Wait until you've tried it before you say that."

They got stuck into the meal, Morgan glad to find the soup really hadn't been ruined and surprised to discover how hungry he'd become. They ate pretty much in silence, passing the odd word about how reliable Waitrose was, what a pain it was to have to go all the way to Okehampton to visit the store, and whether Dominic would prefer his coffee white or black.

With his stomach having stopped rumbling at last, Morgan got up to pour their drinks. "Are you staying overnight?"

"Yes. Halfway between here and Padstow. Through to Monday."

"Oh, right." May Day bank holiday—a lot of people would be making a long weekend of it and the roads back east would be chock-a-block.

"I thought I'd get the best out of the visit, scout out all the possible study sources." Dominic waved his spoon energetically. "There's supposed to be a depiction of the wreck in Quick's. The naval museum."

"There are two. Highly speculative, both of them." That remark was going to sound odd without qualification. "Because, of course, nobody is supposed to have witnessed the shipwreck itself, or to have left a proper account of what happened."

"Yes, I know that." Dominic appeared puzzled. "I wasn't sure how common that knowledge was."

"It's part of our family history. It came with the beams." Morgan moved the conversation on as quickly as he could.

"And how did the beams come here? If you don't mind me asking?"

"On the back of a cart, I guess." Morgan shrugged. "That bit of the story was usually skimmed over. Probably involved my ancestors picking up other stuff they weren't entitled to. Strong tradition of beachcombing among the Capells."

"No doubt. And where there's a will, there's a way, and good strong timbers wouldn't be sniffed at." Dominic drew pictures of mechanisms in the air as he elaborated. "A winch and a pulley? Dragged up the path by a donkey on rollers? The beam, not the donkey."

Morgan sniggered. "Well, however they got them up from the beach, they dried the things out to be used when they built this place. I do know my ancestors stored them away—which might be a euphemism for hiding them along with anything else they got their mitts on—until they were ready to start construction. And as the summer apparently turned cool but dry after *Troilus* went down, the drying out was easier than it might have been. They couldn't believe their luck."

"They must have thought it was manna from heaven if they wanted to raise a house and the necessary material was washed, almost literally, into their hands." Dominic got out his notepad and jotted some notes down. "Lots to be explored, if you don't mind me being pushy and asking further questions. What about the rest of the wreck? I mean, surely other objects came to shore along the coast if the ship broke up? Or are those things lurking in that museum too?"

"I've no idea." Morgan finished putting milk in the coffee and brought the mugs over. "Beachcombing has always been a local hobby, not just for our family, as has hoarding away what you find. Did she have a valuable cargo?"

"I don't think so. And if she did, I don't suppose people were going to confess to finding it." Dominic rubbed his forehead. "So this house must have been built within a year or so of *Troilus* going aground?"

"The next summer. Which was another dry one, surprisingly." Morgan smiled. "We have good weather here on the whole, but I'm sure I don't have to tell a hardened holiday veteran that summer can mean thunderstorms."

"Tell me about it. We always had one or two thundery days— usually right after we arrived. The lightning seemed to come from nowhere." Dominic laughed. "My mum used to say it was coming down in stair rods, but I never dared ask her what she meant. Our home was modern, so I'd never seen one, not until I went to some reproduction nineteen twenties cottage at a museum in London. It made sense then."

"The delights of the impenetrable English language."

"A lot of it comes from the Age of Sail. Sorry. You probably know that."

"I know a bit. 'Room to swing a cat' was the one which confused me as a child—I used to imagine some poor moggy being whizzed around by its tail." Morgan grinned. "I must have been an annoyingly literal child. So, when's Quick's museum on your agenda?"

"Later this afternoon, I think. I'll look at those pictures, despite the fact they're not accurate. I'm not after precision in them, simply the feeling they might evoke. Another layer to the research."

"You'll find plenty of layers, certainly. And as much as you've ever wanted to know about tides and currents and the Devil's Anvil—the stuff about geography and oceanography, or whatever you call it, should be pretty accurate." Morgan decided the coffee was as hot as it was likely to get. "*Troilus* isn't the only ship that's foundered off these shores. Others are bigger or better known."

"So I understand. But the others don't really interest me. Not like she does." The glint in Dominic's eye spoke volumes; there was more to this than fond memories of childhood places.

"Is there some personal connection between you and the ship?"

"Do you usually go around reading people's minds?" Dominic sat back, leaning on the side of the carver chair and cradling his drink. "You talked about your great-great-whatever ancestor and that piece of rock. My great-great-whatever-uncle was captain of *Troilus*."

"Good God." Morgan steadied his hands on the edge of the table. "Well, that was a lucky guess. Or maybe an unlucky one."

"Neutral, I'd have said. I'm not sure I believe in luck, despite the sailing background."

"Were any other members of your family in the navy?" Morgan busied himself with his own drink. He'd read about Captain Edward Watson of the *Troilus*, who went down with all hands, and simply to think of the ship's crew gave him shivers. In his nightmare, he could hear their drowning screams above the roar of the storm, see the bodies battering on the rocks. He clasped his hands around his cup in a vain attempt to steady them.

"His nephew followed the old man into the profession, but then my family parted ways with the sea. One of my however-many-great-uncles was in the merchant marine between the wars and the rest of our history, military or otherwise, is strictly territorial." Dominic took another swig of coffee. "This is good. I'm being spoiled."

Morgan smiled, despite the nausea in his stomach. Dominic was a genuinely nice bloke; why couldn't he have been interested in a different ship, another set of rocks?

"That's a lovely picture." Dominic nodded towards the family grouping on the wall. "Taken in the dining room?"

"Yes. I'm afraid Dad's no longer with us and Mum's . . . Mum's in a home. Only me here now."

Dominic flushed. "I'm *so* sorry. I don't want to intrude."

"No offence taken. It's good to talk about them. Dad would have been fascinated by all your history stuff."

"Can I do a rubbing? Of the marks on the beams, I mean?" Dominic had turned a brighter red.

Oh yes, gaydar's gone ping. Fortunate that Dominic wasn't really James's type or the rat would likely have another broken heart to wear on his sleeve.

Morgan nodded. "I don't see why not. So long as you don't mind a bit of dust."

"You should see the state of my flat." Dominic drained his coffee quickly, as if he hadn't intended what *that* remark might have implied, either.

"Come on, let's get you set up." Morgan pushed back his chair and rushed them round the awkward conversational corner. "Which ones did you have in mind?"

"The ones in the dining room." Dominic got to his feet and grabbed his bag.

"Shouldn't be a problem. Come and show me what you need."

The logistical issues became obvious as soon as they were in the room. The table could be moved, even the sideboard could be shifted at a pinch, but Dominic, tall as he was, would still be short of the beams themselves by a good few inches. "Ah. I think I'm going to be too vertically challenged."

"Silly sod. I'll get the stepladder out of the garage, and you can shin up it with your brass-rubbing kit or whatever you've got in that bag. I guess you came prepared."

"Hey, don't put yourself out. You've gone to enough trouble already without me rearranging your house."

Morgan *had*, but he could go a step or two further. He didn't mind helping the bloke along, especially if faffing around with the beams steered them clear of discussing the wreck itself. "If you're going to do a job, you have to do it properly, don't you? Get your stuff ready and I'll fetch the ladder."

When Morgan got back, Dominic was laying all his kit out on a cloth on the table; neatly, like a surgeon might have his instruments prepared for an operation.

"I'll put this here and you can get on as you like." Morgan propped the steps up against the fireplace. "There's the washing up to do."

"I should be doing that." Dominic looked up, last piece of paper in place. "Go on, leave it for the moment. I could do with another pair of hands here, anyway."

Morgan wasn't going to argue. Any excuse to leave the domestic duty he liked the least; one of the advantages of being with James was that they'd justified using a dishwasher. Why the hell did he have to keep thinking about those days? He shook himself, mentally and physically. "I can manage a pair of hands."

They got on with things, Dominic—meticulous without being fussy—producing a series of rubbings which illustrated the marks on the beams and threw up some Morgan hadn't realised they possessed.

"You should do all of them at some point," he said, as they carefully rolled up the sheets of paper. "I wish I could offer you the run of the place this afternoon, but I've got to be in Padstow later."

"You've gone beyond the call of hosting duty for one day." Dominic smiled. "But if we could manage another time before I fly home, I'd be really grateful. Can I take a rubbing of the stone in the garden too?"

"Help yourself. What about coming back tomorrow afternoon?"

"Perfect. Only don't lay on tea. It should be my treat. Take you out somewhere."

"That's a deal." Morgan left the steps where they were; no point in heaving them up and down like a tart's knickers. "Okay, this washing up. I'll take your offer—do you prefer to wash or dry?"

"Wash, please."

"That's the correct answer as far as I'm concerned."

Back in the kitchen, Morgan happily cleared the table while Dominic ran the water and fought with a slippery washing-up liquid bottle.

"You know, sitting at that table, I had no idea there'd be such a stunning view of the Devil's Anvil from here. Would you mind if I took some pictures from the garden before I go?"

"It's not that different a view from the one you got down on the cliff path." Morgan winced, realising how stupidly defensive his voice sounded.

"Oh, right." Dominic winced like a spaniel, unsure why its owner has snapped at it.

"I simply meant I didn't want you to waste your time. If you were expecting to get something quite different." Now Morgan was being pathetic. How could he begin to explain without having to go through the whole story about why he got so anxious about his old bedroom? How he'd seen this view from there all his childhood years, when he'd had the room above the kitchen, but at the point when he'd inherited the ability to choose where to sleep, he'd moved to the biggest bedroom. "You can see for yourself when we've done," he said, with what he hoped was a reassuring smile.

They did the washing up in a silence only broken by discussion of whether something was rinsed enough and where to put the gloves. When the last suds had gurgled down the plughole, Morgan ushered his guest towards the back door, guilt at having been rude yet again overcoming—albeit grudgingly—his reluctance to go and look out from this angle, even in broad daylight.

It was all so bloody stupid. Face your fears, wasn't that how you were supposed to tackle things? Or was the latest wisdom that you kept a stiff upper lip, like they'd expected in his parents' time? What with James and the wreck and his parents, and the worry that those nightmares might start anew, he needed a whole packet of starch for his lip, plus some whalebone.

They walked across the garden, over to the hedge which marked the boundary on the seaward side, Dominic fiddling nervously with his camera.

"Maybe I misled you." Morgan tried to appear lighthearted. "I don't think I ever realised how much better the view is here, rather than down at the cliff. The extra few yards of elevation add a lot."

"It certainly does." Dominic, clearly relieved to be back on a level conversational keel once more, flashed him a smile.

"I'll let you get on with your photography. There are some late tulips I should deadhead while I remember." There was always something in the garden to make yourself busy with if you needed an excuse to think. This garden had been his mother's pride and joy, and he kept it as well as he could, the gardener who'd been coming for donkeys' years deserving most of the credit.

"Nice millstone." Dominic's voice, suddenly at his back, made Morgan jump. He'd been lost in memories of helping his mother plant these tulips, and time had slipped past.

"Cool, isn't it?" Morgan smiled. Another thing the family had acquired along the way, now decorating the garden rather than hard at work grinding corn. "Oh, before I forget. Do you want me to tell you the route the locals use to get into Porthkennack? It'll avoid the weekend traffic snarl ups and save you time."

"It might cost my life, given what the country lanes are like round here. I'll stick to the main roads, with the rest of the tourists." A small, awkward gap in the conversation ensued. "You've put up with a lot, letting me invade your house. I'm not sure my buying you tea and cakes tomorrow can settle the bill."

Morgan hoped he wouldn't offer money; better to jump in now, before the level of awkwardness racked up. "If you want to, you can buy me a pint this evening."

"Great idea." Dominic beamed. "Why not let me go one better and buy you dinner? I mean, you've saved me a pile of research and everything."

"You insist on paying and I'll refuse to come," Morgan replied, smiling. "Go halfers and I'm happy. When and where?"

"Half five outside the yacht club work for you? I hear it's been tarted up, so it should be a decent enough place for me to wait if you get delayed."

"Yep. Works for me." Morgan consulted his watch, with deliberate theatricality. He needed some time to get his head together before this afternoon's ordeal. "Sorry, I'm going to have to get my skates on."

"Oh, right. My fault." Dominic backed down the path, patting the ballast stone as he passed it. "I'll see you later."

"You will." Morgan watched him all the way out of the gate, feeling guilty about the fuss he'd made about the view from the back of the house. Fucking *Troilus*. Why did that ship insist on haunting him?

CHAPTER THREE

organ parked his car in the carefully maintained car park of the carefully maintained nursing home. This had once been a private house, seeing action in the Great War as a place for officers to recuperate, but the family who'd owned it had run out of money and luck. The recent incarnations of the property as a hotel had been unsuccessful, but the adaptations involved had made it an attractive prospect for conversion. Everything about the building and grounds suggested quality, decency, good taste—it seemed someone was intending to impress the visitors, as well as the residents, remembering that those visitors, whether healthcare professionals or relatives, had some hold on the purse strings.

He looked around at the other cars, wondering if everyone else visiting today felt the same guilt at having had the person closest to them confined, even if it was for their own good. Every newly washed window of the house hid faded dreams, hopes for a long and happy retirement dashed by something which all the money in the world couldn't buy off.

Back in the days when he had shared James's flat in Victoria, the pair of them working all hours God sent during the week so they could have the weekend together, they'd been devising a strategy for what they'd do when they had enough in the bank to throw in the towel and live a little.

That time had been six months of bliss and making plans, before Morgan's father's death had set the domestic dominos slowly tumbling both in London and Cornwall. Funny how you could go along, step after small step, without realising how far you'd gone and how far you'd eventually end up from home. Dad's death, Mum's descent into dementia, the recurrence of his own childhood nightmare, James's infidelity. Milestones on a journey neither Morgan nor his mother had asked to take.

Maybe they could have—should have—expected dementia to strike, but not so early. Morgan's great-grandmother had lost her faculties with devastating rapidity, although the fact she'd been in her seventies meant it had been excused away.

"She had a good innings, not surprising she went a bit gaga given what she suffered losing both her brothers during the Great War." No end of people had said it, blaming everything on the past, in the same way as her daughter's—Morgan's maternal grandmother's—death in a car accident had been put down to what she'd suffered during the Blitz.

Morgan had wondered, with the benefit of hindsight, whether his grandmother's rapid switch from "little old lady cautious" to a Formula One style of driving had been a symptom of the same affliction that was to strike down her daughter. A similar, devastating change in character. The family had shrugged it off as stress related, the consequence of grandfather passing away. Maybe there was some truth in it for mother and daughter, the sudden death of a loved one tripping the last wire in their brains.

Morgan tried not to taunt himself with what-ifs. If they'd been able to predict that his mother might go downhill so swiftly, when she'd only just turned sixty, what could they have done to prevent it? There wasn't yet a pharmaceutical magic wand available to wave.

But it had felt like losing both parents, although the loss of his mother was being drawn out, a continual nightmare from which only her death would bring release. At times Morgan wished that his parents had gone together, so that she wouldn't have had to deal with the consequences of bereavement. Or, perhaps worse, known the frustration and sheer terror of something inside her going wrong and having no idea what it was or what to do about it.

He glanced up at the building once more, abruptly aware of how long he'd been sitting, thinking. Time to bite the bullet—maybe today would be one of the miraculous times when the fog cleared and his mother would smile and they'd talk like nothing had changed and for a short while the world would be a better place.

He found her sitting in the lounge, evidently enjoying the sunshine. The place was clean, well furnished, and didn't have that all pervading "urine plus boiled greens" smell that nursing homes usually did. He'd done some design work for another home, the other side of Newquay, and had hated both times he'd had to visit the place, changing his clothes the minute he'd got through his own door, although the aroma had still seemed to cling to him.

"Hello, Mum." Morgan thrust a bunch of flowers out, feeling like a little boy again, bringing home daisies he'd picked in the lane on the way back from school. "See, your favourites. Alstroemeria. You always chose these."

"Thank you, love." She reached up to caress his face as he bent to kiss her cheek. Maybe this was a good day. "I'm afraid the ones you brought yesterday didn't really last." Not such a good day, perhaps. Morgan hadn't been in for a week, and the last time he'd visited, he'd brought his mother chocolates. "Dad not with you, then?"

Clearly a very bad day, if she'd forgotten *he'd* never be able to visit anyone again.

"Not today. You know him, always busy." Morgan had got used to conjuring up answers. There was no point in telling the truth and distressing her; better the plausible lie. He took the seat next to hers, facing a large picture window with a view of the well-kept gardens.

Mum shook her head. "That bank runs him ragged. I should have a word with Miss Charlton."

She could remember the name of her husband's old boss, even if she couldn't remember his death. They carried on the conversation as though the family connection with National Westminster was alive and well, Morgan amazed at how his mother could recount the detail—accurate detail, as far as he could tell—about things which had happened fifteen or twenty years ago. Yet the present, when they touched on it, was nothing but a muddled blur.

They chatted amiably enough for a pleasant enough ten minutes before an edge in his mother's voice put Morgan's guard up.

"James not here, then?" Funny how her thoughts—and moods—could swing so dramatically and so quickly. The consultant had explained it was typical of this type of condition, part of the deterioration of her mental faculties. It made medical sense, but it still hurt.

"No, Mum. Not this time." Thank God James wasn't there, that he'd never visited this place, and not simply because Morgan didn't want anyone who could remember his mother in her pomp seeing the shell of a person she'd become. This was a personal, strictly Capell tragedy.

"Maybe it's as well he isn't. We don't want any of his kind hanging around." She glanced slyly towards the door out into the corridor, then spoke with a crudeness she'd never have used when she was well. "There's one here, you know. One of the nurses. He watches the men all the time. Dirty bugger."

"Have you seen the doctor today?" Morgan asked, desperate to change the subject, despite the fact that strategy had rarely worked with his mother, memory loss or no. There was a doggedly determined streak in her that had never gone away.

"No. The doctors don't like coming here. They're frightened of that nurse. He might try to touch them."

What wires had crossed in her brain to spark such a dramatic change? Mum had always been so supportive of Morgan, absolutely accepting what he was, making James as welcome, maybe more welcome, than Eddie's girlfriend had been. Was this really a case of a U-turn in personality brought on by dementia, or the truth coming out at last? The revulsion with which she described the male nurse was staggering; had there been times she'd looked at Morgan and felt disgust?

"I'm afraid I'll have to go in a minute." Cowardly, to cut and run, but there was a limit to what heart and soul could endure.

"No! Don't go. You only got here a minute ago." She grabbed his arm, surprising strength in her wiry hands. "Are you afraid of that nurse? I won't let him touch you. I won't let him touch my boy."

"It's not that, Mum. I've got to go to the bank and see Miss Charlton." Morgan, grateful for the inspiration, hated the lie, but sometimes he had to be pragmatic. His mother would never know truth from lie again.

"Tell her from me that she's to stop treating your father like a doormat. Bloody spiteful cow."

This new frankness was unnerving. "I will tell her, don't you worry." Morgan wagged a finger.

"I know. You're a good lad." Smiling, she patted his arm.

Best to end the conversation with a spot of the truth, to salve Morgan's already bruised conscience. "You mentioned James, earlier. I'm afraid he isn't around at the moment. I wanted you to know." Morgan spoke as nonchalantly as if he were informing his mother that the morning paper hadn't yet come. "We've decided to go our separate ways."

"Oh, that's a shame." She shook her head, maybe some strong recollection kicking in of how much she'd liked James. "Did his firm move him to New York?"

Dear God, where had that nugget come from? When he'd first brought James home, there'd been talk of his company relocating him to their American offices. It had been a real threat to their burgeoning—and at the time so promising—relationship. How could she access such trivial facts and forget so much of importance?

"No. They changed their minds about New York. We're not really friends now. Grew apart." He felt like a boy yet again, coming home and telling Mum how someone had been mean to him in the playground.

His mother smiled and patted his hand, like she'd done back then, although she didn't have the standard soothing accompaniment of lemonade and biscuits that had always featured at home. But the smile and the touch were a sign of grace, a small remembrance of things he'd thought had gone forever, forming a benediction on their parting, letting Morgan slip away, without further argument and with happier thoughts than the ones he usually wrapped himself up in as he left her. He walked down the corridor, had a quick word with the nurse on duty, took the lift, then got himself out of the security doors.

The usual relief that he'd survived the visit without turning into an emotional wreck—or not too much of one—and that he was free for another few days, hit halfway across the car park. Morgan consulted his watch; plenty of time to drive into Porthkennack, park and get down to the yacht club, with a bit to spare. He had to get his head in gear before he'd be in any state to be civil to Dominic—the bloke didn't deserve having a heap of angst dumped on him. Morgan never liked meeting anyone straight after he'd been to see his mother, but this time it couldn't be helped. Life had to go on.

Although why couldn't it simply rewind and go back to how peaceful and easy things had been two years previously?

CHAPTER FOUR

Dominic was waiting, as arranged, on one of the benches on the seafront at Porthkennack, overlooking the sea and basking in the sunshine. It was well gone five o'clock, although the air remained balmy and any threat of rain had scudded off to the east with the clouds. It felt more high summer than unpredictable early May.

"I always think of Porthkennack being like this," Dominic said, when Morgan was still ten yards off, as though they were picking up a conversation only just put down. "I always assume that when I return it'll turn out to be a trick of the memory, but the weather's great again."

"It saved its best for you. You should have been here last week, because it was raining cats and dogs." Morgan took a seat on the bench; his favourite nerd didn't look like he'd be moving anytime soon.

"I wish those had been here when we came as a family," Dominic said, pointing at the row of anchors and other nautical works of art placed along the front. "My parents would have loved them."

Morgan nodded. This area used to be an eyesore, all along the esplanade, before the rejuvenation had started. Now it had the stylish appearance it deserved. "I used to feel sorry for all those people at the yacht club, with their view over a load of rotting tat. Not that any of them have got their boats within miles of here."

"It's the beer, not the boats, they come for." Dominic stared up at the wheeling and darting gulls. "They never change. Determined to dive-bomb your pasty."

"If I had my way, I'd have the lot of them shot. Horrible things. Worse than grey squirrels. Give me a nice well-behaved sparrow any day."

"I call them tree rats." Dominic laughed. "Mind you, I call pigeons air rats."

"What are seagulls, then? Air foxes?"

"Too nasty to be foxes. Or pigs. Definitely pterodactyls." Dominic made a gun with his fingers, miming taking down some of the bigger specimens. "When I was small, I used to complain if anything changed. Too fond of what I knew."

Morgan chuckled. "Maybe that's the sailor coming out in you. My dad used to read a lot of Patrick O'Brian. He used to compare me and my brother to Jack Aubrey's crew. We liked what we were used to. Or maybe that was from his Genesis tape. We knew what we liked and we liked what we knew."

"Something like that. Talking of unnecessary change, is the knickknack shop still at the end of the high street? I used to save up my money to have a splurge there at the end of my holiday. It was like Aladdin's cave." Dominic's eyes shone with boyish enthusiasm. "I used to get rocks and snow globes and all sorts of stuff that I'd turn my nose up at these days."

"All you'll get now are things like a skinny latte with an extra shot." Morgan wrinkled his nose. "Sorry to be the bearer of bad news, but it's a Costa."

"Oh. That's a pain."

"Maybe that's for the best. You'd probably have hated the place if you'd seen it through adult eyes. Kids don't notice the tackiness or the chipped paint." Still, Morgan could remember how magical it had appeared to him as a boy, like some of the other now long-gone tourist attractions. He wouldn't think any the less of Dominic for such nostalgia; it was another shared connection.

"I guess you're right. You usually are." Dominic stretched, yawned, and leaned back. A strange feeling of old camaraderie settled over them, as though they'd known each other years. Cornwall was like that—it was always easier to relax and just be content in this county, rather than in London, with the atmosphere of continually striving to succeed.

Minutes—although it could have been half an hour, given the peaceful ambience and the liquid quality of the time—passed before they spoke again.

"Sorry, I must be holding you up." Dominic unexpectedly leaped from the bench. "We should go and eat."

"Sounds good to me. Not that you *are* holding me up, but my guts are complaining. Did you have anywhere in mind?"

"Anything would suit me. You choose, given that you'll have the inside knowledge of what things are like now. I'll likely take us to a pub and it'll have converted to a Tesco Express."

Morgan snorted, though that was too true to be funny. "Do you like Italian? Or would you prefer Chinese? Indian? Fish and chips?"

"I like anything, as I said." Dominic suddenly shut his eyes and spun around, like a little boy, just as suddenly stopping and thrusting out his arm. The dreadfully polite-sounding, dreadfully English tourists on the next bench studiously ignored the mad pantomime. "This is what we used to do when I was young. Whichever direction I'm pointing is where we go."

"Out at sea, at present. Got your budgie smugglers?" Morgan laughed. "It's a shame you weren't pointing towards Padstow. My favourite eateries are all in that direction."

"We could cheat. I wouldn't tell."

"Nah, it's daft getting back in the car when I've only just parked up. Either you can spin again or we can use Shank's pony. I know a nice shabby-chic bistro if you don't mind ten minutes' walk."

"Make it so," Dominic said, with a theatrical sweep of the hand and a huge smile.

Morgan smiled in return, lost for words. Maybe he'd been blind when they'd first met, or maybe he was so low in spirits at present that he lacked judgement—but now he realised Dominic wasn't bad looking at all. With a broad smile and the sun lighting up his hair like an aureole, the bloke was dead fit. Morgan would have to tell his hormones to control themselves, because falling into a rebound relationship—assuming Dominic *did* turn out to be gay—always ended in tears.

Morgan would keep the conversation on strictly nautical lines, avoiding anything potentially like flirting. It would bring them back to *Troilus*, but any awkwardness about the ship—and the possibility that Morgan's nightmares might edge into the conversation—would be less tricky to manage than romance. He led the way along the esplanade, Dominic falling into step beside him. "Any luck at the museum?"

"Yes and no. There was a painting of the wreck, but it's totally inaccurate. Wrong type of ship for a start—I'm not convinced there ever was a frigate that size, not even a razee, if you know what they are."

"I do." Morgan had read all about *Indefatigable*, when he'd fancied the pants off the actors on the television version of *Hornblower.*

"I knew you were bright. Anyway, the painting was produced in late Victorian times, so it must have been based on a report of a report of a report." Dominic gave a *pfft* of evident disapproval.

"Right, so that's the no. What's the yes?" Morgan stopped by the side of a busy road—busy by Porthkennack standards, at any rate. "Wait. Tell me on the other side. I don't want you being pulverised because your mind's two centuries away."

A snarl up at the junction ahead, where somebody had parked inconsiderately, allowed them to slip between the stationary vehicles.

"There seems to be a bigger volume of traffic here than when I was a child." Dominic frowned, clearly put out. "And nothing seems as cheap as it did then."

"There is and it isn't." Morgan snorted. "I'm not crabby enough to say it's been ruined—plenty of things are an improvement on what they used to be—but it *has* changed."

Dominic caught his eye. "Maybe I shouldn't complain too much, in case you start to think I'm a grumpy old git."

Morgan resisted any comment; almost anything he could say in response might smack of that flirting he was trying so hard to avoid. He stopped in his tracks. "You still haven't told me the yes part about the museum. Shall I lie in the street, kicking my legs and screaming until you do?"

Dominic laughed. "You'll get no dinner if you have a tantrum. And you'll embarrass me so much I'd refuse to tell you."

"That strategy never worked when I was a child, either." They walked on.

"The yes," Dominic said, continuing seamlessly as they crossed another little road, "is a name. John Lawson. He was a midshipman on *Troilus*, and he's of real interest."

"Why him in particular?"

"I've read that he was a favourite of the captain. Various people have taken that to mean he was a natural child, which is part of what I'm trying to find out. Perhaps the most important bit." Dominic stopped at a small crossroads. "I don't remember coming up here. Which way now?"

"Just cross and keep going straight on. It's only fifty yards ahead. You're in Porthkennack locals' territory now, off the grockle trail." The rumble of cars and the chatter of families was fading behind them. "Keep going with the story too."

"Officially Lawson was the son of a friend of the captain's wife. That's how he was given a place on the ship—although he'd been signed onto the books for years before he once set foot on the decks. They called it sea time back then."

"I have no idea what that means, and don't elaborate. I'll google it." In spite of his reluctance to think about real sailors, like the crew of *Troilus*, Morgan had to admit that Dominic was piquing his curiosity.

"You do that. Anyway, if Lawson was a by-blow, the captain wanted the child close by him. Family story is that he couldn't support or acknowledge him in the normal way of things, so he had to help him along informally."

"Interesting. I wonder if his wife knew?"

"Only if she was watching from her cloud. *She'd* died after a long illness following a miscarriage. Young John was born a year after, possibly a result of Captain Watson taking a little comfort when offered it. Although he never married again, so there's a story in itself."

"There is indeed." They came to a halt beside the bistro. "Don't stop just when it's getting interesting."

"I won't. Although I need feeding first."

"We'd better hurry up before your stomach deafens me with its rumbling." Morgan held open the door to usher them in. The next few minutes were taken up with being squeezed onto the last remaining table, then ordering drink and food.

"This other woman, John's mother, couldn't have married Captain Watson," Dominic continued once the waiter had taken their order.

"Because she was already married?"

"Got it in one. To an old duffer who loved her dearly but couldn't give her a child, if the tales are right." Dominic leaned closer and lowered his voice, clearly aware that the two middle-aged ladies at the table next door had started to hang on their every word. "Probably couldn't oblige at all in the bed department, which is why she might have turned to Captain Watson when she saw her chance."

Morgan caught the ladies in mid-gawp, smiled at their embarrassment, then said to Dominic, "Lawson was her husband's name?"

"Yes. Mr. Lawson had made his money in the sugar trade, but there was naval blood in the family. She was the sister-in-law of an admiral, which is how she got to meet my ancestor."

"At some posh ball? Shades of *Pride and Prejudice*?" The allusion to Jane Austen attracted attention from the table next door again.

"Nothing so fancy. Mrs. Lawson and Mrs. Watson hitched a lift on *Troilus*. The rest, as they say, is history."

"History or conjecture?"

"A bit of both." Dominic cast a glance at their nosy neighbours, before evidently deciding that if they wanted to listen in, they'd have to put up with what they heard. "Here's something odd. I found a letter. Or I should say a copy of part of a letter among a collection of bits of correspondence. Stuck in an old commonplace book or scrapbook or whatever, that my grandfather had from his grandfather. It was supposed to be from Captain Watson to his mistress."

"His mistress? Mrs. Lawson?"

"Probably. There's no name, not a term of endearment, although enough references to make it pretty certain."

"Like what?"

"Like fond memories of the ladies being on *Troilus*." Dominic smirked. "I assume she didn't take to his cot there and then, as that would have caused a scandal given the presence aboard of his lawful wedded wife, and risked the possibility of Mrs. Watson smacking Mrs. Lawson with a blunt instrument."

"The women in your family sound downright scary."

"Protective of their own."

The waiter appeared with their drinks and—thank goodness— the bill for the table next door. If they were that bloody nosy about a bit of scandal concerning a pair of naval wives, what would they have done if Morgan started talking about James? He and Dominic shared a grin as the women paid and left.

"Talk about scary women." Dominic jerked his thumb towards the now-empty table. "Could they have leaned any closer?"

"Maybe they thought you were discussing current events. Some poor Captain Watson, ex-RN, now living down in Padstow, whose reputation is about to go up in flames." Morgan picked up one of the breadsticks which had arrived with their drinks, then broke it. "That's how rumours start. Perhaps the same thing happened with *your* Watson. Old biddies half heard a tale and spread it."

Dominic, halfway through consuming his own breadstick, shrugged. "Could be. Or old sailors. They gossip just as much. That's the problem with a lot of research—picking fact apart from speculation. Or downright lies."

In that case, conducting research was no different to running your love life. "Any facts at the museum?"

"There are some factual items of uniform. One of them is a pair of midshipman's flashes, like they'd have worn on their collars to show they were the lowest of the low." Dominic licked some crumbs from his fingers, with evident relish. "The speculation bit starts with the labelling. There's an account next to the exhibit stating the items had belonged to Lawson. No explanation as to how the person claiming that knew for certain, just the bald statement. Which begs about a dozen questions, especially since nobody is supposed to have survived."

"Are you absolutely sure that was one of the genuine items?" The museum was a whimsical place, run by people with a peculiar sense of humour. Several of the rather capricious exhibits presented legend almost as if it was scientifically proven truth—the kind of thing the grockles would lap up—and unless you filtered the lighthearted from the serious, you might come away with some peculiar ideas. Like believing mermaids were real.

"I'm absolutely sure of nothing, but the name is a strange coincidence. The official records say he went down with the ship, so how could his uniform have ended up there? And in good condition, rather than ripped to shreds on the rocks where she foundered?"

Morgan took a long draught of Perrier. "And are official records always correct?" he asked, as neutrally as possible. Today had proved easier than expected, so maybe he was getting acclimatised, or whatever psychologists would call it when you faced your problems.

Dominic doodled with his finger on the table. "Better than most, but they are what they are. People fall between the cracks of the written accounts. I suppose most of the sailors who died never had the privilege of any grave but a watery one. If they washed up in some secluded bay, they might never have been found until—"

Morgan held up his hand. "You don't need to go into details. Especially not before a meal." The thought of a body lying on a beach, at the mercy of flies, crabs, and gulls, didn't bear thinking about. "Why is this story so important to you and your family? You talk about having to find the truth. Is this about Lawson's parentage?"

"Not quite." Dominic lowered his voice again. "If Lawson survived the wreck, he was on that ship to start with. In person, and not just in name. Agreed?"

"Agreed."

"In which case he couldn't have been killed by Captain Watson before the ship set sail."

"What?" Morgan almost dropped his glass.

"That's the rumour. That Lawson found out who his real father was, then started to put pressure on Captain Watson to acknowledge him." Dominic doodled on the table again. "Watson, with the connivance of his officers—who couldn't stand the lad—had him killed and buried in a remote cove."

"Is there any proof of this?"

"Not a scrap, apart from a letter to the newspapers written by one of Watson's old enemies. It caused a heap of trouble for the family, besmirching his good name. I'd love to clear him."

"Of course you would. If our midshipman survived, we need to prove it beyond all doubt."

Although when had Lawson become *their* midshipman?

CHAPTER FIVE

Sunday dawned bright. A new morning always raised Morgan's spirits, and this one felt particularly promising. Normally the day after a visit to the nursing home saw him on a short fuse, but his temper had steadied itself after the meal out. This morning he'd potter around—do some gardening, do some work—then Dominic would arrive, with all his kit and caboodle. And no doubt another pile of questions.

Dominic had come out of his shell the previous evening, no longer the strange creature who'd made the original phone call. Now the thought of him coming back to discuss *Troilus* was no longer quite so daunting.

By the time Dominic came knocking on the door, Morgan had ticked off his list and was feeling pretty chipper. Chipper enough to leave his guest to get on with taking rubbings of the ballast stone while he put the kettle on. He'd even, in another moment of generosity which surprised him as much as the recipient, told Dominic that he could take a small sample from the boulder, from the point where some of it had flaked away, if that would be helpful.

"I have no idea *what* would be helpful for my research, so I won't refuse the offer." Dominic's grateful smile proved an unexpected reward for the offer.

Once the sampling was done, they took tea and cake out in the garden, perching on the bench and basking every time the sun revealed itself.

"Can I ask where the house name came from? *Cadoc* strikes me as a bit odd. I mean it's odd to us 'foreigners.' Sorry. Is that rude?" For whatever reason, Dominic seemed especially awkward today.

"Does it have any significance? Apart from this area being near St. Cadoc's point?"

"No other significance that I'm aware of. I know Cadoc was the name of a local king or an earl or something. My guess is that one of my ancestors just liked the sound of it."

"Ah. Gotcha."

"There's a lot of Capell history and, like with your sailors, it isn't easy to pick apart hard fact from embroidered fact. Or from downright fiction."

"Par for the course. What *do* you know for certain?"

"Not a lot. The original family home was west of here on a field like the great north face of the Eiger, or so my great-granddad used to tell my mum." Morgan closed his eyes, in bittersweet reminiscence of family members long gone and much missed. "That old place fell into disrepair when Queen Victoria was a girl, and eventually the family moved to the house here, where some of the Capells had already made their home."

Dominic screwed up his eyes, mental maths evidently in action. "If that's true, how did your great-grandfather know about it?"

"Family stories. There wasn't a lot to do here for entertainment apart from make cider and tell tales. Probably at the same time." Morgan had spent many happy hours enthralled by the family raconteurs. "And he'd been taken to see the very field, although it no longer belonged to us. I can take you there, but I can't promise there's much to see that would be relevant to your research."

"I'll take your word for it. Cadoc it is, then." Dominic pronounced the name as no local would have done, but Morgan wasn't going to correct him. "And *you've* always lived here? Apart from the time in London," he added hastily, as though he was aware of having made a faux pas.

"All my life, apart from three years in Cardiff at uni. Then another three years on and off in London." Funny how he'd been so keen then to get away from the confines of Porthkennack. Cardiff had been revelation enough, but London itself had felt like Paradise. Yet the capital had ended up feeling more confining, more stifling, than this little headland ever had. Or maybe it had been James doing the stifling? "But you know that."

"I'm not sure I know much about anything." Dominic frowned. "But from your expression, I think I've prodded the elephant in the room. Sorry."

Not the main elephant, but certainly one of the herd. What had Dominic been told, and how had James explained his familiarity with the private story of the beams? "What did James actually tell you about me and him?"

Dominic, forehead crinkled in thought, stared out towards the sea. "Not a lot. Your James doesn't give much personal stuff away."

"Hm. Well, he's no longer *my* James, so I'd prefer you not to call him that." Morgan's short fuse made its presence felt at every mention of the rat.

"Sorry." That flaming word again. "I didn't realise things were quite so touchy. He said that you'd parted as friends."

Morgan snorted. "I bet he did. He might well have believed we were. Hold on." He smelled another rat, apart from James himself. "*When* exactly did you meet him?"

"About a week before I rang you. I know it sounds daft, but it took me ages to work up the courage to get in contact." Dominic gave him a glance. "We were both at a big promo do at an art gallery. James's company had done work for them, and my lot were one of their sponsors. I got dragged along to do my corporate bit, bored stiff until I found a modern watercolour of Cornwall. James seemed as interested in it as I was."

Dominic gave an account of the chat with James, the audit trail of words and ideas by which conversations moved and ended up elsewhere, how discussion of childhood holidays in the West Country had turned to adult obsession with wrecks, but Morgan was only half listening.

He'd done his own mental maths—a week before Dominic's phone call, he and James had still supposedly been an item, if living apart to see if absence rekindled the flame. The bastard, to say they'd already split up. What if Dominic had rung Morgan the next day after the meeting and referred to James as "your ex"? The rat would have appreciated not having to break the bad news himself.

Dominic, wincing, said, "Sorry. I've clearly put my foot in it somewhere."

Why the hell did Dominic spend his whole life apologising? "Stop fucking saying sorry." He took a deep breath. "*You've* nothing to apologise for. Unlike James. I wasn't aware we'd split up at the time he met you."

"Ah. Sor—" Dominic put his hand to his mouth. "Maybe it's best if I go." He reached down for the rucksack which lay at his feet.

"Oh, for fuck's sake, there's no need. You shouldn't suffer because *he's* such an A1 arsehole." Morgan managed a smile.

"At the risk of putting my foot in it again, I must confess that—now I've met you—I'm surprised you two ever were an item."

"Why?" Morgan's hackles rose again. "I could pull the city slickers in my heyday."

"I never doubted you could," Dominic said, with a sudden grin. "You've got the looks and probably the knack. I never had. It's just that James . . . Would you mind if I was entirely honest?"

"I would find that refreshing."

"Okay. It's just that James seemed such a slimy git, it amazes me you put up with him. You could do much better for yourself."

Morgan found himself lost for words. That was the last few years summed up in a sentence. He shrugged, and got another smile in return. "That's exactly the confidence boost I needed right now. Thanks."

"My pleasure. Not that your private life is any of my business, and not that I have anything sensible to say about it, given my useless romantic record. My experience could get written large on the back of a postage stamp." Dominic shrugged.

Morgan found himself torn between saying *Don't do yourself down* and *Stop fishing for compliments*. He rejected both as too flirtatious, settling for, "Want to go and see the Devil's Anvil a bit closer up? Tide's pretty well as far out as it'll go."

"Can you doubt the answer?" Dominic let Morgan take his arm and pull him out of his chair. "Especially with a local guide to show me the things I might have missed."

"No pressure on me to get the facts right, then." Morgan grinned and let go his guest's arm, the sensation of Dominic's silk shirt still haunting his fingers. Dominic produced yet another of his stunning smiles in return.

Those exchanged glances were undoing all Morgan's resolve.

The familiar cliff edge always seemed less hazardous on a still afternoon like this one, despite the notice warning people of the dangers of going too near the edge or attempting the path in bad weather. It led down to the little sandy bay, tacking across the cliff face in a series of natural and uneven steps, all of them showing their age; nonetheless, it appeared inviting.

"I wonder how many people carved that trail, treading the grass away over the years?" Dominic stared at the drop down to the sand.

"Too many. Let's add another two, though." Morgan led the way, sure-footed from years of making this descent.

"Do you think all those people thought they were the first to discover this place?"

"Maybe." The idea appealed at some deep level to the explorer instinct. Being the first to tread virgin sand, to have found the wide pool that got left when the tide ebbed; the right to say, *I came here first. I claimed it.*

"They'd all have been wrong, of course," Morgan continued. "People must have been walking here since the caveman came along and fancied a dip. I can't believe the local Stone Age folk confined themselves to flint knapping or chasing bears."

"I'd never thought of that. Good point." Dominic eyed the waves, although they were behaving immaculately, about as threatening as a lido. "Isn't it dangerous to swim here, with the rocks and all?"

"Maybe they'd have had a paddle, then. Or a sunbathe, if Neanderthals did that." Morgan, ignoring the last couple of steps, jumped the final few feet onto the sand. "If you feel like swimming, there's a natural pool that people sometimes use."

"Really? I was only ever allowed to play on the sand. Mum was too protective of us." Dominic sat on a convenient rock to loosen his shoes. "And we always seemed to get the tide times wrong, although I suspect it was deliberate. Mother wouldn't have wanted her boy to risk his neck with those rocks."

While his guest bared his feet, Morgan sat thinking. Dominic must, surely, have been on this beach, or up on the cliff path, in summer while *he* wasn't far away, playing in the garden. Or maybe Dominic would have been walking one way along the path while he and Mum took their old Labrador the other way. They'd have passed, like ships in the night.

Ships in the night. Morgan shivered, despite the warmth of the sun. "Not many people are brave enough to use the path any longer, so I get the place to myself when I choose to come here. Although it's still a favourite place with lovers, apparently."

"I can understand that." Dominic peered up the cliff face, shading his eyes. "You wouldn't be seen because of that overhang."

"And the rocks mostly protect you being seen from seaward. Ships don't come too near." Another sudden frisson, this time at the thought of *Troilus* getting too close.

"Sand's soft too." Dominic squatted on his haunches, passing rivulets of sand between his fingers before beginning to accumulate a little collection of shells—winkles, limpets, and something broken Morgan couldn't name. "A bit too public for me, though."

"Glad to hear it." Morgan had never fancied alfresco love. Although maybe that admission had been a touch too much, given the embarrassed smile playing on Dominic's lips. "Right, I'm going to park my arse somewhere not too sandy."

They settled themselves on a wide, flat, comfortable rock, Dominic still jiggling the shells in his hand. "This was always my favourite sunbathing spot."

"Mine too. Dad's favourite, as well."

"Your dad was interested in history, I think you said?"

"Yeah. Among other things. He was a serial hobbyist, dabbling at this and that and changing every few years." The loft contained boxes of old paints, books, postcards, and craft tools that paid testament to his varied pastimes. "Family histories—ours and other locals'—was the last of many."

"Shame. I mean shame it wasn't ships and shame that he's gone. I won't say the obvious 'you must miss him' because that's simply crass."

"Thanks. I do miss him, though. He was the best bloke I ever knew."

Dominic fiddled with the shells again. "Want to change the subject? I'm clearly suffering foot-in-mouth disease."

"Nah. You're okay. What do they say? 'It's good to talk.' James was never keen on getting things in the open, and my brother's just as useless." Morgan gave his guest a grateful smile. "I won't go all blubbery and great wet lettuce on you."

"That's good. I don't mind some big, hairy rugby player crying pre-game when they play 'God Save the Queen' but otherwise I don't cope that well." Dominic started flicking the shells onto the sand. "Anyway, you're wrong about your dad being the best. I'd put him equal with my old man."

"Pillock." Morgan slapped the bloke's arm, sending the rest of the shells flying. "I was being serious."

"*I* was being unnecessarily flippant." Dominic's apologetic grin expressed the word he'd been banned from using. "Trouble is I'm so used to getting the whole sob story—with or without tears—about how awful parents are and how they've made people's lives hell. Times are I've felt guilty that I had it so easy."

Morgan nodded. "Yeah. People enjoy being victims; they like to blame someone else. I know that some guys do get a really rough deal, but I also know that it can just be a line they trail." He took a long, cleansing breath. "I was a pillock too, back when I was a teenager."

"Some might say you still are."

"Ha bloody ha. Anyway, I was worried that my dad would flip his lid when I came out—he'd once mentioned something about a guy he knew at school who was gay and how he'd been beaten up one night on Clapham Common. I got it into my head that he approved of what had happened."

"Bloody hell."

"I worked myself up into a right state. Thought he'd told me the story because he hated queers. Or, worse still, had suspected that I was one and was warning me off confessing it to him."

Dominic closed his eyes, whether against the bright sun on the water or in disgust, who could tell? "So what tipped the balance? Surely you came out to him in the end if you reckon he was so great?"

"Yeah, of course I did. And it was a couple of pints of Chough's Nest beer that tipped the balance by loosening my tongue." It had been a memorable evening, the chat turning out better than the beer, which might have been gnat's pee for all that Morgan could recollect of the actual drinking he'd done. "I'd been a complete idiot, as usual. I was so worried I'd screwed myself into imagining all sorts of crap. It turned out the point of him telling me the Clapham Common story was that he'd guessed about me being gay and was worried I'd end up being duffed over like the other bloke if he didn't warn me about what might happen."

"Oh, what a star." Dominic chuckled. "Isn't that just about the biggest problem in the world, when people don't talk to each other?"

"After world hunger and disappearing megafauna, maybe." Morgan raised a finger. "Don't say sorry. I was being flippant too. Communication may not be the world's most urgent issue, but it causes plenty of problems."

"Yeah. Mind you, if the couples in the average rom com sat down and talked things through rather than jumping to conclusions, there'd be no story line, would there? Nobody could fall into the trap of assuming the fit girl the leading man was cuddling up to was anything but his sister."

Morgan sniggered. "Do you fancy paddling today? I won't tell your mother."

"So long as you keep that promise. She still thinks I'm aged about seven. Says I don't eat enough and should wear my vest. I've not worn a vest in years." Dominic leaped up, grinning. Morgan had been wrong about James casting his line at this particular fish—the rat would never have put up with such unsophisticated enthusiasm. A tug at his arm flushed thoughts of James out of his mind. "Come on, slowcoach."

"Race you." Morgan sped down to the water's edge, sending sand flying.

Dominic, clutching his side, was hard on his heels. "Not fair. I've got a stitch."

"Out of condition, you."

"I need to get back into practice, then. I used to hare along here when I was little. Bloody loved every moment we spent here." Dominic stretched his arms. "I kept pestering my parents, asking why we couldn't move to Porthkennack permanently."

"Organising life always seems easy when you're nine. No obstacles in your mind."

"Too true. My mother used to say we couldn't move down to Cornwall because it wouldn't be an extra special place if we lived here all the time. That was only half the story; I know now it would never have been workable."

"Just as well. Or else we'd be invaded by oiks like you." Morgan smiled, as they diced with the waves' farthest reach. "As I said, my family have always lived in Cornwall. Or at least my father's family have, probably back to the time of the Conqueror. My mother's lot were very new. End of the eighteenth century."

"Practically grockles." Dominic bent to scoop up a batch of pebbles, weighing them in his hands, then leaping back as the water splashed his feet. "That's bloody freezing."

"Too early in the season." Morgan found some pebbles, as well, flinging them out to sea as though they'd carry all his problems away with them. "Dad used to get caught out too. He'd be in here wave jumping almost as soon as spring had sprung. Drove my mum mental." He winced.

"Are you okay?"

"Yeah. Ignore me. Just got a serious case of verbal diarrhoea. All sorts of crap pops out when it shouldn't."

Dominic, nibbling his lip, glanced at him sidelong, then flung a few more stones and waited.

Morgan eventually broke the silence. "It's not been easy the last few years."

"What else happened?" Dominic sent a pebble skimming across the surface of the waves, bouncing an impressive number of times before submerging. "Result!"

"That was a corker." Morgan tried to emulate it and failed. "What happened? Life fell apart. The whole works." There, he'd done it: begun the big admission, and the world hadn't ended. "Dad died, Mum was taken ill. Final nail in the coffin of my ability to cope was splitting with James."

"I'm not very comfortable with touchy-feely." Dominic kept his gaze fixed out to sea and the Devil's Anvil's great jagged grin. "But I'm a good listener."

"I think you've proven that." Morgan kept chucking pebbles; the activity was unexpectedly therapeutic. "Not long after Dad died, Mum started showing signs of dementia."

"Oh hell."

"You can say that again. Bit of a conversation stopper." Chuck another pebble. "When it's a hip replacement or something physical, people are great. They all rally round. When it's in the mind, people never know what to say or do."

Dominic shrugged, tossing the pebbles in his hands. "It doesn't bother me. I can understand; I mean it's not hit me quite so close to home, but I get it."

"Similar thing in your family too?" Here was just a glimmer of hope; a chance he'd finally met somebody he could open up to.

"Yeah. My grandmother. We all felt so bloody helpless."

Morgan nodded. Yeah, Dominic "got it." "I ended up shuttling back and forth for a while, then she got so bad she had to go into a home, just over a year ago. The house was empty for a while, then I started to visit for the odd week or two here and there."

"And what did James think?"

"He was understanding, or at least he appeared to be. I felt guilty as sin, torn between the two places. In the end I found I couldn't stay in London. I came back and began tidying up *her* affairs . . . then found this was where I needed to be. I didn't want us to have to deal with the same sort of mess Dad had left."

"Did James prefer doing a bunk than helping you cope long-term?" Dominic's bluntness was never going to earn him a career in the diplomatic corps.

"In his defence, it wasn't like that. Not quite, anyway. He was really good at the time Dad died. It had been a hell of a shock to all of us." But death was comparatively easy to deal with: serious and conventional and almost dignified. Going senile by degrees wasn't. "It was so sudden. Cerebral aneurism. One day Dad was right as rain and the next . . ." Morgan steadied his hands, gripping the little pebbles to the point his fingers hurt.

"Sudden or expected, it's never easy to deal with."

"I wasn't even here when it happened. I just managed to get down to say a last good-bye, although he couldn't have known me by then. Thank God we'd spoken on the phone a couple of days before." They'd spoken every week, unlike Eddie, who'd been on the blower to their mother every few days, which was ironic given how rarely he visited her now. But maybe that particular closeness had made her decline much harder for him to face. Morgan had always favoured his Dad, and they'd never stopped loving each other—fiercely, protectively both ways. Coming back here and being close to Mum had been a duty Morgan felt he owed his father. No, *duty* wasn't the right word; it made it sound onerous and unwanted. It was more a mark of respect to the old man, carrying out what he surely would have done were he still alive.

"You have my every sympathy." Dominic skimmed another pebble. He must have known exactly what bereavement was like given the pained expression on his face and the catch in his voice.

"While it pains me to admit it, to do James credit, I'd have dissolved entirely if he hadn't been so . . . sensible." And he had been, helping to sort out Dad's monetary affairs, locating the stashes of money in different accounts. Dad had been as much a serial investor as he'd been a serial hobbyist, and he'd been the one firmly in charge of anything financial, so Morgan's mother hadn't known where to start.

Morgan gave Dominic a brief account of James's financial caretaking, including the farcical aspect to straightening out the affairs of a man who'd always sworn he was uncomplicated. "But," he finished up, "we had to return to London eventually. There's only so much leave you can take, compassionate or otherwise. Mum said she'd be fine and we should just leave her to it."

"And you feel guilty about that?" Trust Dominic to get straight to the heart of the matter again.

"Of course I do. I can't help thinking that if I'd stayed on here, if I'd jacked in the old job and concentrated on family matters for a while, then either she wouldn't have got ill or the progress of the disease would have been slower." Morgan found weighing the stones in his hand surprisingly soothing, like they were prayer pebbles. "Think about that sudden weight of responsibility she had to shoulder, on top of the shock of bereavement. I could have helped her to cope better. And maybe she wouldn't have had the fall if I'd been here to keep an eye on things. She took a tumble—in the kitchen, of all places. The room she'd made her domain."

"It would probably have made no difference, you being here or not. She could have taken a tumble in the supermarket or anywhere. I'm afraid it often starts with a fall, the descent into forgetfulness and deterioration." Dominic put his hand on Morgan's shoulder. "I think I'm beginning to see the big picture."

If Dominic really did see some bigger picture, then he was either a step ahead of Morgan or he was about to unleash a pile of platitudinous twaddle. Morgan shrugged the hand away. "And what *is* the big picture?"

Dominic, who didn't seem offended at the brush-off, chucked a handful of pebbles into the sea, as though enumerating his thoughts. "That you liked James a hell of a lot. That maybe you loved him, and you definitely expected more from him. That you'd really like to hate him now, but it's harder than expected. You could find closure easier if you loathed his guts."

Morgan, taken aback, let the little stones slip out of his fingers. "Bloody hell, do you read minds?"

"Not that I'm aware of." Dominic turned, smiling shyly. "When you're used to being among the spectators, you pick up the knack of seeing what the players miss."

"You've got the knack, all right." Morgan rubbed the sand from his fingers; he'd had his fill of opening his heart to public view. "We should walk along to the next bay, around the point, before the tide turns."

"Lead the way." Dominic smiled, happily. A low-maintenance guy, which made a pleasant change.

They walked along the water line, rounding one set of rocks dry shod, then through shallow waves around another, moving circuitously towards the tongue of cliff which pointed out towards the Anvil, beyond which any sane person wouldn't attempt to go except via the cliff path.

"Isn't there a risk we'll get cut off?" Dominic, trying to keep his balance on a jagged boulder as they approached the last bay, seemed to be having second thoughts.

"Not if we make sure we get onto this next little beach. There's another path up." Morgan had kept them moving, pointing out the locations where he'd skinned his knees as a child and the place where they'd had to rescue some stupid holidaymakers who couldn't, or hadn't bothered, to read the tide tables.

They reached the last bay safely, ensuring that their access to the path was clear. Dominic scanned the view, wide-eyed, obviously taking everything in. "We never came down here. What a stunning place."

"Nice, isn't it?"

"Not sure I'd use the word 'nice.' Dramatic, I'll grant." Dominic took another sweep of the bay. "Is this place haunted?"

Morgan couldn't hide his reaction, the almost palpable sensation of a slap to the face. Before Dominic could say anything, he replied, "I'm not sure. I've honestly never come across any ghost stories for these particular bays, which is odd in itself. Standard fare for the books tourists like to pick up, so you'd have thought if there was anything to say, somebody would be making money out of it. Do you believe in ghosts?"

"I believe in a sense of place. Of something remaining that resounds in the air." Dominic studied the Anvil again, that great jagged grin of rocks still seeming to mock them. "Or maybe people bring that resonance with them. Some invisible load they carry."

Morgan bridled. This was all too close to home. "That sounds ridiculous. Like the kind of thing they'd have believed in the middle ages."

"DNA would have sounded ridiculous in the middle ages. And electricity." Dominic's elegantly waving hands illustrated his point.

"Steady on." Morgan pointed up at the cliffs. "Anybody sees you from up there and they'll think you're waving for help. We'll have the lifeboat out any minute."

"Sor— Okay. Getting carried away." He clamped his hands to his sides. "Anyway, electricity. A stream of particles, too small to describe, and impossible to define in terms of their size and position at the same time. Powering everything from a light to a train."

"Bugger me." Morgan smiled, despite his discomfort. "That's quite right; I'd never considered it."

Dominic smiled, knowingly. "There are more things in heaven and earth than you've dreamed of."

"'Than are dreamt of in your philosophy,'" Morgan said, automatically. "Don't quote Shakespeare at me unless you're going to quote it accurately. Tell me about your sense of place."

"Oh, I'm no expert. No firsthand experience to offer in evidence, except for times when I've been somewhere—there's a church at St. Brelade's Bay on Jersey for example—and I've felt the years resonating through the stones."

"I can agree with that." Morgan tried to pick his way through a minefield of words, any of which might raise an awkward question. "We've been to Jersey. And there have always been odd occurrences here too. Not all the weird stuff in Quick's yesterday is a load of cobblers invented for the benefit of tourists."

Dominic laughed. "Just ninety percent, I guess?"

"Something like that." Morgan returned the grin. "But a lot of it's in the mind. I was driving home one night along the back roads and ended up almost crapping myself. There was something huge ahead of me, nearly twice the height of the average man, and it kept glowing in the headlights. Intermittently, which was worse still."

"And?" Dominic's eyes were wide now, full of anticipation.

"It was only someone out on a late horseback ride. Got both themselves and their mount covered in those reflective safety strips. I felt a complete idiot." Morgan laughed. Keep it light and he might steer clear of making an idiot of himself again. "Stupidly mundane, a product of my susceptibility and overactive imagination. I keep thinking that if I'd turned off the road before I'd established what the cause was, all the rest of my life I'd have believed I'd seen a ghost. Maybe my story would have ended up in the museum too."

Dominic smiled. "I suppose there are plenty of things that spook people for which there's a rational and boring explanation. Will-o'-the-wisp. Ball lightning. But *do* you believe in ghosts?"

"I've no idea whether I do or not," Morgan said, hoping that they'd get off this bloody subject soon. "Can we just leave it for the moment? I'm not in the mood to discuss superstitious nonsense."

"I'm sor—" Dominic theatrically slammed his hand over his mouth. "I'll stop flushing elephants out of the bush, okay?"

"Okay. You're all right." Morgan patted his shoulder. No need to make the bloke feel worse than he already did. "Come on, we should be getting to the top before the tide comes in or the wind strengthens."

Dominic eyed the cliff face up and down. "I can't help wondering if John Lawson could have got up there with the wind blowing a gale and the rain lashing."

"John Lawson?"

"Our midshipman. The one who might just have survived. Remember?"

"How could I forget?" Although that name had slipped Morgan's mind for the moment, probably because of all the other thoughts flooding his consciousness.

Dominic ran his slender fingers through his wind-tousled hair. "He must have had help, given the terrain."

"What if somebody saw the ship foundering and came down to help?" Morgan shivered, even though the sun was warm on their backs.

"Are you okay?"

"Yes, I'm fine." How long was he going to be able to get away with pretending?

"I know it's bloody rude, but it strikes me that you're *not* fine. And it's not about your dad or your mum or ghosts or anything remotely like that."

Morgan opened his mouth, then shut it again. What would it achieve giving Dominic a gobful of defensive abuse? The guy must have noticed the odd enigmatic remark and would have started constructing the crossword from the little clues, putting in all the right answers. He was too shrewd by half.

"I can see you're angry, but just listen to what I have to say. I promise that if you shout at me, or go so far as to smack me one in the gob, I won't think any the worse of you." Dominic looked pained and sounded as awkward as he'd done during that first phone call. "Something about *Troilus* bugs you. *Really* bugs you."

The predictable topic still made Morgan wince.

Dominic frowned. "See? That's exactly the kind of thing you do every time I mention it. I've been pretending not to notice, but I can't any longer."

Morgan considered arguing, but what was the point? He took a deep breath, blew out his cheeks. "Am I that obvious?"

"Too right you are. Sometimes you flinch and sometimes you simply put the shutters down behind your eyes. If that makes any sense."

"It does." Morgan sighed. "I just don't want to talk about it at the moment. If ever, to be brutally frank, but that would bugger up your research and I said I'd help."

Dominic frowned. "Okay, I take the hint. Should I clear off and take my research with me?"

"Don't be sodding stupid. You keep offering to treat me—why don't you get dinner?"

"Great idea." Dominic's face brightened. "Hint taken. Subject officially changed. And I'll drive. You've earned being chauffeured."

"Only if you let me direct you down the short cuts. I can't face the holiday traffic."

"Deal."

And please God they wouldn't encounter anything on the way to remind them of ghosts or ships or nightmares.

CHAPTER SIX

Morgan heard the house phone, as it bleated out through an open window, as soon as they reached the garden, but he wasn't quick enough to reach the thing. The fact there were two answer phone messages already suggested that someone desperately needed to get hold of him. Heart sinking, he felt his pockets, realising he must have left his mobile on the hall table. The messages—as he'd already anticipated—asked him to ring the nursing home.

"Sorry, got a call to make." He made an apologetic face at Dominic, who, with a sympathetic smile, headed off towards the kitchen.

The news from the home wasn't good. His mother had suffered a fall, if only a minor one, as the sister reassured him, which was no reassurance at all. If the incident was so minor, why the string of messages, both on the home phone and—he saw as he checked it— the mobile?

"We've popped her down to Newquay hospital for an X-ray, but it's simply a precaution." Christine, the sister in charge who Morgan often saw when he visited, sounded her usual breezy self, although it didn't allay his fears.

"Do you want me to get down there?" Guilt at not having been in the house to answer the phone, and having left his mobile behind, fought with guilt at hoping Christine would simply tell him not to bother.

"No, we just wanted you to know what had happened, in case you came visiting and found she wasn't here. Didn't want to have to rush *you* to the hospital with a heart attack because of the shock." The forced jollity in Christine's voice alarmed Morgan more than her words did. "We'll ring you if anything changes. I tried your mobile, but I couldn't get a reply on that either."

"I know. Sorry. I went out for a walk; must have forgotten it. Been a bit preoccupied."

Christine's voice changed to one of professional concern. "That's all right. We understand. Your mother wasn't at her best yesterday when you saw her. You must have been upset."

"Yes." He'd leave it at that. "You promise you'll be in touch straightaway if I'm needed? I'll make sure I have my mobile phone with me all the time."

"Of course. Go and make yourself a cup of tea or something. And don't worry."

Don't worry? Might as well ask that tide not to come in.

"I've put the kettle on, if that's okay. Everything all right?" Dominic asked, poking his head out from the kitchen.

"Yes. No. God knows." There seemed no alternative to explaining what the call had been about. Morgan finished up his account with the question that bugged him. "If they're insisting the situation isn't serious, then why did they keep trying to ring me? I can't help thinking that they're lying."

"Unless they were covering their backs. In case you'd have thought about suing them if anything *had* happened and you'd been the last to know. Compensation culture and all that."

"You could be right, but I'm not convinced." Morgan glanced at the phone again; the instrument seemed to be mocking him, piling the guilt on.

"If you'd rather not go out to dinner, I'd understand." Dominic looked around the hall. "Let me get my gear together and I'll head back to the hotel."

"No!" That had been too loud, too desperate. "No. Let's have that cup of tea. Help clear my head a bit."

"Yes," Dominic said, clearly needing no further explanation. "Maybe some biscuits would help too."

"I'll go have a rummage in the cupboard."

Dominic had the leaves in the warmed pot, and Morgan had run a decent packet of biscuits to ground when the house phone went again. Morgan ran into the hall to grab it, his stomach sinking before he even registered Christine's voice at the other end. Once he'd heard everything she had to say, he turned to find Dominic hovering in the kitchen doorway.

"The nursing home?"

"Yeah." Morgan gave a helpless shrug. "I have to go down to the hospital. This fall's shaken Mum up badly, and she keeps asking for me. That tea will have to wait."

"I'll run you down there." Dominic moved across to the table where he'd left his keys along with his camera. "I can wait and bring you home, or you can get a taxi back. You'll be in no state to drive either way."

Morgan, about to argue, suddenly realised there was nothing to fight about. His hands were shaking, and he didn't feel too steady on his feet. Why not, for once, take a well-meant offer? "You're on. Get your stuff together first, though. I'm not trying to get rid of you, but it could be the middle of the night before I get home, and you don't want to forget something."

They occupied themselves with domestics, making sure Dominic had collected all his gear, that Morgan had cash, cards, and mobile— and a coat in case he had a long stay, coming out into a cold night. Concentrating on the practical rather than what really occupied his mind: what would the situation at the hospital turn out to be?

Once in the car, they focussed on negotiating the back roads, avoiding the tourist trail, and trying not to knock any grockles off their bikes. Dominic seemed as determined as his host not to discuss the present crisis. They eventually pulled up near the hospital, after what seemed an age of short cuts which had turned out to be anything but.

"You'll be all right?" Dominic asked, eyeing the emergency department entrance.

"I'll be fine, honest. I'm sure things can't be as bad as my brain's trying to tell me they are." Morgan forced a grin.

Dominic touched his arm. "I can be flexible with flights. If it would help to have someone around to fetch and carry or whatever, given that you can't be sure what's happening. I won't get under your feet at the hospital, but I could stay in the area and be your spare pair of hands. Seriously."

Morgan flipped a mental coin. Heads: Insist he'd be fine, say that Dominic should go home to London and he'd be on the blower when he had some news. Face this on his own as he'd got used to facing stuff on his own. Tails: say, *That's what I need right now—been a long time since anyone's looked after me.*

Tails it was.

"I can't think of any jobs for you to do at the moment, but I'd be really grateful to have someone here. To help prop me up." There, he'd committed himself. And it felt good. "You won't have a problem reorganising flights, if you need to?"

"I doubt it. My father happens to be on the board of the airline."

"Is he?" He'd kept that quiet. "Magic. Thanks." Morgan had opened the door and was halfway out of the car before he remembered his duties as a host. "I don't know how the hotel's fixed for accommodating you another night, but it seems a shame to put you to extra expense when I've got a spare room. Come and stay with me tomorrow. We might be able to get out for that meal, if everything's hunky-dory in there."

"You're on. Ring me with an update."

"I will. Hope to see you some time tomorrow."

Morgan watched the car drive away before he headed for the hospital entrance. Had that invitation for Dominic to stay been solely motivated by hospitality? Or had there been something else lurking there, something he didn't want to admit to himself?

He found the entrance to the accident and emergency department, and made his way to a desk where he had to wait while they processed what looked like a holidaymaker whose arm had suffered a close encounter with a sharp object.

"I'm Mrs. Capell's son," he told the receptionist, once it was his turn. "Is she all right?" Stupid bloody, typically English question. Of course she wasn't all right or why the ambulance dash to casualty?

"She's gone through. I'll give them a ring to find out what's happening."

Morgan waited, increasingly frustrated as he listened to half the conversation and tried to guess the rest. At last, the receptionist addressed him.

"You can go through now. They're expecting you."

"Thanks." Morgan followed the signs, picking a trail past patients, relatives, paramedics, some of whose bank holiday weekends were clearly turning into a nightmare. He found where he had to go, being greeted by a young female doctor with a tired but welcoming smile.

"She needs a period of observation, that's all. She came down with a bit of a bump, but we don't think she'll need to stay in here longer than overnight. She'll be as well looked after in the nursing home." The doctor led him past a row of curtained cubicles, through a door, and into a small side ward. "You might want to prepare yourself for her appearance. There's a fair bit of bruising on her arm."

Fleeting thoughts of horror stories about nightmare care homes and the abuse they'd given the people in their care flitted through Morgan's mind but were put onto the back burner. He'd had no suspicions on that front, heard no whispers; if there were any problems, the Porthkennack gossip machine would have been trumpeting them. And if bruising on the arm was all he had to prepare himself for, then he'd be happy.

"Will she really be okay? You're not trying to fob me off?"

"Yes, she will, and no, I'm not. There's nothing broken. They say she needs a lot of rest to let everything recover. It takes a little while at that age, you know." The doctor smiled again, exuding a no-nonsense, reassuring air, although Morgan wasn't comforted by it. He couldn't shift his guilt at the fact he and Dominic had been arsing about on the beach when the accident had happened.

"I'll leave you to it," the doctor said, as they reached his mother's bed. She was asleep, peaceful, with a childlike contentment on her face. "There's no hurry at the moment to discharge her. We'll chat again later."

"Yes. Thanks." Morgan took a chair, settling himself down before getting his bearings in the ward.

The woman in the next bed appeared frail, paper thin in places, as if a puff of air might blow her away. Thank God Mum still had a wiry strength about her, still looked as though she might walk out of here and go back to Cadoc practically unaided. The bruises were nowhere near as bad as Morgan had imagined, and when she was resting quietly like this, it seemed hard to believe she wasn't the same woman who'd often been asleep in a deckchair in the garden only a couple of years previously.

How could an illness that changed a person so entirely leave so few external signs?

The effects of the day's drinks were making themselves felt, and he'd best use the facilities while his mother was out for the count. He found a passing nurse, got directions to the visitors' loo, and found welcome relief.

As Morgan washed his hands, he studied his reflection in the mirror; the face he saw was exactly the same as when Dad was still alive, if pale and drawn after the rush to get to the hospital. How could the traumas of the last few years have left so few marks on him too?

Late Monday morning, after a reasonable night's sleep, Morgan got on the phone as promised.

"Hel-lo?" A cheery voice sounded down the line.

"Dominic?"

"Who else do you think would be answering my mobile—some hunky bloke I picked up last night?" Dominic snorted. "How are things?"

Morgan smiled; it was good to have one point of constancy and humour in his life. Dominic had come along just when needed. "Mum's fine. Badly bruised but nothing broken. She was surprisingly lucid once she woke, despite the shock and the painkillers. I stayed with her until the ambulance came to take her back to the nursing home."

"I'm glad to hear that. All round."

"Thanks. It was a relief that the drugs didn't make her more confused."

"Yeah. I've only been on morphine once and I wouldn't want to repeat it. Off my face and propositioning the doctors." Dominic laughed. "I was getting a bit worried when I hadn't heard from you. Thought the news might have turned serious."

"Yeah, sorry about not ringing earlier. Didn't get home until the wee small hours and then I simply crashed straight out." And then some. Morgan had been out like a light until half ten this morning; he couldn't remember the last time he'd slept that well.

"Hey, don't you say sorry if I'm not allowed to!"

"Touché." Morgan chuckled. "What are your plans for the day?" Did that sound too hopeful or too desperate? Too late to take it back.

"I'm doing some extra research, of course. All the areas I'd have been investigating if you hadn't been distracting me with biscuits and beaches. Working my way through some old papers and maps I brought here and seeing if they stand up against the evidence of what's still here. Might give me a hint of their overall reliability."

"Good thinking. Much of this place hasn't changed over the years. Certainly not the basic geography." Morgan felt a bit jealous—he'd have liked to go along and help with that research, but the biscuits and beaches and the hospital run had left him with a pile of unfinished jobs too.

"I know. It's stuck in a time warp. I've got some Edwardian pictures that could have been taken yesterday. Um, are we still on for dinner tonight? If you're not too tired, of course."

"Yes, we are. And I'm about to make sure the guest bedroom's aired and made up. What time will you get here?"

"Is midafternoon all right? I think I'll have done what I need to by then."

"Perfect. I'll have the kettle on."

"You and your teapot—that's an offer nobody could resist." With another laugh, Dominic hung up, leaving Morgan to get into host mode.

It was good having a bed to make up and dusting to do, plus a dozen little domestic things which helped Morgan keep his mind off his mother. Thinking about Dominic helped too. The bloke had changed—the nice, kind, relaxed bloke in the car hadn't sounded like the stuffed-up guy who'd first made contact. If the one who'd driven him into Newquay was the real Dominic, then Morgan was really glad he'd be hanging around another day.

The nursing home rang after lunch to say she'd had a good night and was now awake, eating well, and in pretty good nick, considering. They advised him not to visit for a day or so, to let her settle back down again, which was a weight off his shoulders.

He threw himself into work—his as yet unattended emails another good way of keeping his mind occupied—until the doorbell announced his guest's arrival.

"Afternoon." Dominic's bright smile as the door opened soon turned to an expression of concern. "You look awful."

"Thank you so much. You missed your calling in the diplomatic corps."

"Sor . . . Oh hell, if I can't use *that* word, what am I supposed to say? 'Many apologies for having overstepped the normal boundaries of decent conversation'?" Dominic grinned.

"Come in, you bloody idiot."

"Do I still deserve a cup of tea? I'm parched." Dominic dumped his bags in the hallway.

"I'm not sure you do, after that remark about how I look. I've been working hard to make myself presentable." That was a lie, a flirtatious lie; Morgan felt strangely elated.

"You don't need to work at that. You'd be presentable at three o'clock in the morning, stumbling out of a club and into the gutter."

"I'm not sure that's a compliment, either." Morgan rolled his eyes. "But I'll take it."

"I seem to be talking myself out of that cup of tea." Dominic hung his head in mock shame.

"You are such a plonker." Morgan ushered them into the kitchen, before busying himself with kettle and pot and all the paraphernalia. "Did you get anything to eat last night?"

"Only in the hotel bar, but it was okay. Didn't feel much like going out. How about you?"

"I grabbed a snack at the hospital. Something out of the vending machine. I didn't fancy eating at all, but Mum nagged me. Funny how she still worries about me not eating enough."

"That's how mothers are. We're always stick thin to them." Dominic looked out of the window, clearly relishing the sea view. "So I owe you this meal. If you're still up for it?"

"Yes," Morgan said, with more enthusiasm than he felt. The prospect of an intimate tête-à-tête in a restaurant with all the world and his wife at hand loomed up like an ordeal he didn't want to undergo.

"Having second thoughts?"

"Must you mind read? I'm feeling a bit tired and emotionally bruised, that's all. Could do with some fresh air, as well. I can't rid my nose of the hospital stink."

"Eau de carbolic?" Dominic blew out his cheeks. "You know that I'm always happy to get out. And not just to do my research—you've got to make the most of the seaside when you're heading back to London."

"Been there, done that." Morgan studied the contents of the pot; at last the tea was ready to pour. "Sea air it is, then. And any chance you'd settle for fish and chips or something equally mundane afterwards? To be eaten here where I could stagger to the couch and crash out at two minutes' notice if the great tiredness descends? I appreciate it's not the big meal out you must have had in mind."

"Don't worry. I'm easily pleased." Dominic blew on his tea, taking an appreciative sip. "Cracking cuppa. Want to see what I've turned up?"

"If it's maps and photos, then yes. No ship talk, though."

"Wouldn't think of it. Local geography of a strictly land-based nature, it is."

Soon the dining room table was covered with maps and old photos, some of them kept in place with the now-empty mugs, while Dominic's laptop had been set up to display the pictures he'd taken over the last few days. Morgan had filled in a few of the gaps from the Capells' collection residing in his sideboard, including a trove of picture postcards of local views which had been his father's. The Devil's Anvil and the Long Cove featured prominently, but those jagged rocks didn't seem anywhere near as threatening seen in a four-by-six postcard.

For a nerdy activity—something James would have sneered at—it was good fun. Morgan sighed. "I wish you could have met Dad. He'd have bent your ear for hours about local history. I'm not sure how much would have been relevant to your research, but it would have amused you."

"This is excellent background material, though. I've never seen these specimens before." Dominic angled some of the older cards to the light to get a better view of them. "I've got plenty of the standard local ones, Padstow and St. Enodoc church and the rest of the tourist trail."

"Why not take some of the less common ones with you? As a memento of your visit."

"I couldn't. Not if they were your dad's." The eager, yearning expression in Dominic's eye gave the lie to his words.

"Of course you could, you numpty. He had loads of them, doubles of most. There must be more boxes up in the loft. And he'd have preferred them to go to a genuine enthusiast rather than any old riffraff via the charity shop. That's why I haven't cleared them out." Morgan chose a couple of the least dog-eared old postcards. "Here. Actually . . ." he scooped them all up, "have the lot. I've plenty of other pictures, and the sea views I can look at any day, out of the window."

"Are you sure?" Dominic beamed like a little boy at Christmas, fingers itching to get themselves on the goodies.

"Absolutely. Do you want to see any of the other stuff he collected, or would that bore you rigid? The sideboard draw's full of this, that, and the other. I have no idea exactly what he crammed in there."

"Bore me?" Dominic's eyebrows shot up. "How could anything about Cornwall bore me?"

Morgan resisted the temptation to say that pretty well everything about Cornwall had bored James. Why keep thinking about him now? Or at all? He had to come to terms with a James-less life and the sooner that happened, the better. "You may live to regret saying that, when we're on the seven hundredth view of St. Enodoc church and golf course."

"If I yawn even the once you can whack me."

The day had passed into early evening by the time they got out for their walk, but it had kept the best of the sunshine for them. They parked in a private road, where a friend of Morgan's allowed his pals a closer access than the grockles got.

Morgan had always loved the view from the Long Cove, especially at times like this, when the setting sun slipped down the sky the other side of the headland and set the distant waters aflame with dancing light. He liked it when the flowing spring tide came dashing up the beach, crashing on the rocks and threatening to soak any poor souls who went too close to the water's edge. But he loved it equally when the tide was on the ebb, leaving a broad expanse of sand and, if you knew where to seek them out, rock pools like he'd delighted in as a boy. Then he could walk along the strand for ages without seeing more than a handful of other souls, at the right time of year.

He'd always hoped that James would have fallen in love with it too, but he'd preferred the busier, tamer sands at Rock and Newquay, with their accompanying restaurants, bars, and Kensington tractors. Surely Dominic would never show the same preference? Morgan now felt it vital that Dominic would genuinely like the places he liked and not pretend to be enthusiastic from politeness. They parked the car, got out, then took a deep breath of salt-spiked air.

"This is my favourite part of the headland," Dominic said, out of the blue, shading his eyes against the sunlight flickering on the waves. Was he always going to have a direct line to Morgan's thoughts? "We used to walk along here for hours, one way up top on the path, then back the other way in the surf."

Morgan looked up and down the bay. "I can't decide whether I like the surf or the rock pools best. I found my favourite shells here."

"Did you? I seem to remember all the shells I came across were right grotty specimens." Dominic glanced sidelong at him. "Have you always been lucky?"

"I wouldn't ever describe myself as lucky." When James had come along, Morgan had thought himself the most fortunate man in the world—how things changed.

"That's how it should be. Or else any hubris will surely lead to a fall. Better to be the way you are. I like it." Dominic favoured Morgan with a smile, one of those devastating, unexpected smiles, then scrambled down the bank by where they'd parked and onto the path. Morgan, like a sprinter stuck in the blocks when he thought that someone else had false started, eventually followed him. They risked the sand—they could always shake out their shoes—walking slowly, watching the last of the holidaymakers, talking intermittently, enjoying the silences in between. Not one mention of ships or parents or ex-boyfriends, just the latest stories to have topped the local news, how the area still seemed, in places, stuck in the nineteen fifties, and a series of increasingly exaggerated boasts about their best beachcombing finds.

Lost in conversation, they almost forgot to turn back, finally reaching the car as the light was on the ebb.

Dominic slapped his hands over his stomach. "Sorry for that noise, but no apologies for using the word under the circumstances. It wasn't thunder. Stomach thinks my throat's been cut."

Morgan smiled. "Mine's not far behind. I'm glad it's chips on the menu; I'm so bleeding knackered I couldn't face a restaurant wait."

"Chips sound like caviar to the intestines."

"If that's supposed to be a clever joke on Hamlet, it failed."

The drive to the Salt and Battery fish and chip shop—the food was better than the cheesy name—didn't take too long, which was as well given the accompaniment of stomach rumbles. They didn't bother with taking them home and warming them through, consuming the gourmet treat with wooden forks straight from the paper. No Michelin-starred restaurant could have served them better. And no shared candlelit glances across the table could have made Morgan feel any gooier inside. The bumping of elbows over the gear stick had sent a tingle up his arm like a jellyfish's sting.

"These chips are spot on. *Better* than caviar as far as I'm concerned." Dominic smacked his lips, clearly savouring a particularly crunchy piece of potato. "That's overpriced and overrated."

"You're preaching to the converted there." Morgan shut his eyes to better enjoy the succulent piece of batter that always graced the end of a cod fillet. James would have turned his nose up at this—he liked his caviar, and anything else expensive and, preferably, out of season. The scales had just about totally dropped from Morgan's eyes.

"Why does anyone bother with posh restaurants when they can have this?" Dominic said, dreamily.

"The only logical reason I can think of is that posh restaurants don't stink your car out. I think I'll need it fumigated to get rid of the reek of fat and vinegar." The smell clung to everything, despite the fact they'd opened the windows as they ate.

"Small price to pay, though."

"Yep." Even if he'd have to pour himself straight into the shower when he got home if he didn't want to wake in the morning smelling like a chippy. "You can't get food as tasty as this anywhere with a Michelin star."

You couldn't sit so close in a posh restaurant, either. It would be really easy to reach over, turn Dominic's face to his and share a vinegar-laden kiss—maybe too easy. No rebound relationships, right? How often was he going to have to remind himself?

"I think I'll smell of vinegar for the rest of my life," Dominic said, conveniently breaking the romantic spell.

"Use the bathroom if you want a shower or whatever when we get back. Make yourself entirely at home." Morgan crumpled up the chip papers, stuffed them into their paper bag, then lobbed the bag in the back. "Hotel Cadoc will soon be ready for business."

Once they'd driven home with the windows part open—freezing them to death but the torture was worth it—the reek had pretty well gone and neither felt the need to go haring off to wash. Morgan busied himself with getting Dominic settled in and showing him the first floor of the house. The guest bedroom, the guest bathroom, the location of the squeaky floorboard that could give you the willies at two in the morning when you trod on it.

"Nice room." Dominic laid his suitcase by the guest bed and placed his laptop case carefully on the chest of drawers.

"It was my brother's. Close the window if you get too cold." Morgan stifled a yawn. "Excuse me. Last night's starting to catch up. I'm going to have a nightcap, I think. Can I pour you one?"

"A glass of white might finish me off for the night. Which sounds like no bad idea." Dominic yawned and stretched; that seemed to put the lid on any chance of romantic activity, which was probably as well.

Nightcaps were soon consumed, accompanied by a bowl of strawberries rummaged out of the fridge and plenty of yawns held back until they refused to be controlled any longer.

"I know it's rude, me being host and all, but I'm about ready to stagger up the wooden hill. Mind if we call it a night?" Morgan rolled his shoulders, fighting aching muscles from where he'd sat hunched at his mother's bedside.

"Not at all." Dominic produced another yawn. "I'm ready to hit the sack."

They walked upstairs in silence, sharing an awkward good night on the landing, as though they both might have something to say and were too tired or too unsure to say it. But like the moment in the car, this one passed without developing.

"Sleep tight, see you in the morning," Dominic said shyly before going into his room and shutting the door.

"See you in the morning."

Morgan smiled, ruefully. He'd convinced himself he didn't want Dominic to make a pass, so why did he feel disappointed? And what would he have done if Dominic had? Given in, probably; there was enough loneliness weighing down on him to make that a goer, no matter how shattered he felt and no matter how much he kept telling himself it wasn't the right thing to do. Dominic wasn't the type of guy you should say no to without good reason. But stumbling into unexpected attraction and stumbling away from James was taking some getting used to.

But the offer hadn't been made and that was that.

Morgan got into one of the T-shirts he liked to sleep in, used the bathroom, then lay in bed listening to his guest pottering about. Dominic made two trips to *his* bathroom so either the fish and chips had upset the bloke's stomach or he'd simply forgotten to clean his teeth. Everyday domesticity, the unexpected satisfaction and comfort of having somebody else in the house, no matter that they weren't in his bed.

These signs of ordinary life, or the sheer fact that he was washed out from the night before, settled him down and drove him into the arms of Morpheus like Usain Bolt up the one-hundred-metres course.

CHAPTER
SEVEN

Morgan woke in a sweat, unsure of where he was or what was happening, apart from the fact somebody seemed to be demolishing the house with a sledgehammer. When he'd shaken himself fully awake, he grasped it was only someone knocking on his bedroom door.

"Are you all right?" a muffled, worried voice asked. *Dominic's voice*, Morgan's befuddled brain eventually informed him.

"Yes. Fine." He sat bolt upright. "Is there a problem with Mum? Did I sleep through the phone ringing?" He switched on the bedside light; the clock said it was just gone half past one.

"No, unless we both slept through it." Dominic didn't wait to be invited in, opening the door and peering round it anxiously. "You didn't sound fine. I thought you were being murdered."

Hell, had he been that loud? "I'm so sorry. I didn't mean to wake you."

"I know that." Dominic smiled, coming completely into the room before perching gingerly on the side of the double bed. "Were you having a nightmare?"

"I'm afraid so." Morgan tried to give the impression it was nothing to get worked up about. "Side effect of excess of those mushy peas, I suspect."

"Probably as bad for you as cheese. You look like death warmed up." Dominic patted Morgan's leg through the duvet. "Want me to make a cup of tea or anything?"

"No, or else I'll be having to get up again to use the loo." Morgan forced a smile. "Actually, I tell you what might help. Could you stay here a while? Only for company."

"Of course I can, so long as I can slip under the covers. It's getting bloody freezing out here." Dominic shivered; whether that was accidental or done deliberately to emphasise the point, Morgan wasn't sure. He wasn't sure if this was the start of a pass, either. Still . . .

"Come on, then. Can't let guests get cold." Morgan edged across, freeing the duvet and letting Dominic under it, although he kept his distance.

Hell, it felt like an eternity since he'd had anyone other than James to snuggle up (or wrestle) with. If this turned out to be a fledgling night of passion, it was like none Morgan had ever known. Instead, it was as though two schoolboys were having a sleepover and discussing ghost stories in the night. *Ghost stories.* Morgan shivered at the thought.

"You must be freezing cold as well." Dominic felt Morgan's arm. "Bloody hell, you're like ice. Come here." He grabbed Morgan's left hand, rubbing it between his. Dominic's fingers were strong, adept, and hugely comforting. "It must have been a pig of a dream to leave you like this."

"Tell me about it," Morgan said, immediately regretting his words. "Here. Warm the other one." He turned, slipping his right hand into the reassuring grip.

"What you really need is a roaring fire. Or a cuddle. I can't offer the fire." Dominic freed his hands, slipping his arm round Morgan's shoulder to take him into a wiry but gentle embrace. "The only way to stop parts of you freezing off."

Morgan could think of another more effective and more appealing method, and maybe he'd been wrong to think his guest wouldn't have the same thing in mind. If this was an attempted seduction on Dominic's part, it was certainly endearing, if clumsy and clichéd. In character, then.

"Thank you." Morgan sighed, happily leaning into the embrace.

"Thanks for what?" Dominic hugged him closer.

"For melting this here iceberg. I thought I'd never be warm again."

"It's what any half-decent friend would do." The hug changed, Dominic's fingers now wandering lightly across Morgan's shoulder.

"What about a lover?" Morgan turned his head up so he could peer into his guest's eyes, having one last rethink before they crossed the bridge over which there'd be no going back. "What would a lover do?"

"What a stupid question. He'd do this." Dominic leaned in for a kiss or three. Soft tender kisses, firm longing kisses, desperate needy kisses. No further words for now, only two mouths—and bodies— beginning to familiarise themselves with each other.

Dominic proved surprisingly skilful, touching and caressing with assurance and style; the bloke was good at this. He was so adept, and eager, that Morgan soon lost any guilt that he might be forcing his guest into doing something he only had half an inclination to do. And that he might be getting himself into something which wasn't a good idea in the long run. He needed comfort tonight, and he'd work through the consequences, whatever they were.

"I'm going to sound mad, but I'll risk it. I usually sound mad, anyway." Dominic whispered against Morgan's neck as they stopped to take a much-needed breather. "I've fancied you since you first appeared in view on Saturday, haring down that path like there was a fire to put out."

"I was running because I was worried you'd go too far and end up over the cliff." Such a bizarre concern, looking back. "Don't ask why, I just got it into my head that some terrible accident might happen. That if you were a stranger who didn't know the dangers, you couldn't be trusted . . ."

"Do you trust me here? In this bed?" Dominic's voice had taken on an authority it hadn't carried before, not even when he'd been talking about his beloved research. Maybe in the bedroom he found his truest metier. "I promise I'm safe as houses. Safer than ships," he added, kissing Morgan again.

"Then I'm putting myself in your hands."

Morgan did so—literally and figuratively. He wasn't disappointed, innocent kisses and caresses soon sailing the seas of passion and into the dangerous waters of abandonment. He wasn't going to mind what they did or how they did it; he wasn't expecting the romantic encounter to end all romantic encounters.

"What do you fancy?" Dominic asked, as they broke from a wonderfully stimulating clinch.

"What have you got?" Morgan would take anything at the present moment, and Dominic would have to be sharp about it. Excitement was reaching fever pitch, and Morgan didn't feel inclined to keep it under control.

"Whatever you want. I'm flexible. In more ways than one."

"You say the most romantic things," Morgan laughed. "Surprise me."

Which was exactly what Dominic did, showing an adeptness with hands—and tongue—that Morgan would never have predicted he possessed. And Morgan had never realised how stupidly exciting it was to be stroked on one particular spot on the tender skin between his legs, a spot which Dominic found with unerring accuracy.

Release came quickly, and with a careless pleasure Morgan had long forgotten was possible. He gave as good as he got, revelling in the delight of discovering what worked and didn't for this new and unexpected lover.

"That was good," he said when they had both got their breath back, snuggling down at Dominic's side, determined that the bloke wasn't going back to the guest room for the rest of the night.

"Only *good*? I must be out of practice." Dominic laughed gently. It had probably been a minor miracle he hadn't said sorry when they'd been rolling between the sheets, but in the sex department he'd had nothing to apologise for.

"Maybe we should organise some further chances for you to get into training, then." Morgan, wonderfully sleepy, gave his guest a good-night kiss. "See you here in the morning, gorgeous."

"Yeah." Dominic returned the kiss. "Hope the bad dreams have all gone somewhere else now."

"So do I." Fucking hell, didn't he just?

Morgan had managed to get back to sleep very easily, only to wake again fighting for air and coughing, as though expelling water from his lungs. He panicked at finding a body next to him, a split second of incomprehension followed by happier remembrance.

Dominic started, then woke. He grabbed Morgan's arm, sounding increasingly concerned. "What's the matter?"

"Nothing. Only a touch of indigestion. I'll be fine." That didn't sound convincing. Why did the dream have to come back tonight of all nights, and with such recurring vengeance? All the talk of *Troilus* the last few days must have stimulated parts of Morgan's brain which were best left fallow.

"It isn't 'nothing.'" Dominic got out of bed, slipping on the T-shirt he'd discarded so easily earlier. He switched on the bedside light. "Have you had another nightmare?"

"Yes. How the hell can you know? I'm starting to think you're psychic."

"It's bloody obvious, from the same 'rabbit in the headlights' expression you had earlier. The same face you wear when we talk about *Troilus*." He sat on the bed, taking Morgan's hand to rub it, and swopping the hard edge in his voice for something lighter. "I'm starting to think you're having nightmares just to stop me from sleeping."

"Pillock." Morgan glanced up at the window, unsettled. Had the curtains not been drawn, he still wouldn't have been able to look out to sea—this room faced inland—but the Devil's Anvil kept calling to him. "Okay. You've got me bang to rights. It isn't the mushy peas. It isn't the business with Mum unsettling me."

"That's been obvious too." Dominic squeezed the hand he held. "Don't talk about it if it makes things worse." Trust him to have to sprinkle everything with an apology, even if it was in his tone rather than his actual words.

"It doesn't hurt to talk. Not with you, anyhow." Morgan sighed.

You've trusted him with your body—why don't you trust him with your mind?

Good question. Nobody, not least James, who'd been a damn sight more intimate body-wise, had been allowed access to the darker recesses of Morgan's thoughts. Maybe it was time to get it all into the open. He nudged Dominic's arm. "Want to go downstairs and get a drink? Somehow I don't fancy going back to bed and finding I either can't sleep or I nod off and the dream comes back."

"We don't have to try to sleep." James might have said the same thing, but he'd have been distinctly lascivious, trusting that sex would solve any problem. Which it never did.

"We don't," Morgan replied, returning the squeeze. "Except this wretched nightmare's knocked my libido for six. Sorry."

"That's my word," Dominic said, leaning over and kissing him on the forehead. "And we're both banned from using it remember? A drink it is. Want me to get the kettle on?" He grabbed a rug from the end of the bed and enfolded himself in it like a cloak.

"Sounds like a plan. I'll find my dressing gown." Bugger, it was perishing tonight, like November rather than May. "You get in the kitchen, and I'll put the fire on in the lounge. No point in catching our deaths of cold, like poor sailors washed up on the rocks."

"No," Dominic said slowly, giving Morgan another sympathetic smile.

Obviously the cat was at least half out of the bag. Might as well release it entirely. "I'll tell you downstairs."

Morgan soon got the lounge cosy, with a couple of table lamps lit and the imitation log fire turning out warmth and light. Just like his childhood days: fire, hot drinks, some blankets from out of the cupboard under the stairs, ones left there from when they'd been used to wrap poorly children. Comfort all round. If Morgan wasn't in a situation where he could tell everything now, he never would be.

"I used to have the bedroom that you're in." Why not start by giving Dominic some context? "You'll have an amazing view over the sea tomorrow."

"I did wonder if that was the case. There are some old things in the cupboard where I hung my jacket, which I thought might be yours."

"Are there?" That showed how much Morgan avoided the room.

"I also wondered why anyone would give up such a stunning view. I guess you're going to tell me." Dominic blew on his tea before sipping it appreciatively.

"Something weird happened to me in that room when I was about seventeen. I relive it, in recurring nightmares—usually when I least want to." There, that wasn't so hard to confess, was it?

"Want to tell me about it?"

"No, I don't. But I will." Morgan took a deep breath. "It's odd. Sometimes the whole thing feels like it happened to someone else, then the dream recurs and it's all too real."

"Then tell it like it happened to someone else. See if that helps."
Dominic nodded, cradling his mug and waiting patiently.

"All right. One night, Morgan got out of bed and went to the
window. He looked out through the trees . . . Oh, this is bloody
stupid." He punched Dominic's arm.

"Steady on! Don't spill my tea."

"Sorry. *I* looked out." How to capture how peculiar that night had
been? Some faint light from the westering sun had still been catching
the top of the waves; grey water, with a northerly wind whipping
up the white horses. "I was watching the sea, when a storm came in.
That sounds clichéd, the old 'It was a dark and stormy night' thing,
but that's exactly what it was like. Eerily dark, like I was staring into
a barrel of pitch. The wind rattling the windows and rain howling.
I used to like storms, from when I was a little boy, watching the sea
scudding and the birds taking shelter and me feeling snug inside."

"Rain's a great thing to watch from the other side of the window."

"I always thought so, but I've changed my mind since that night.
That was different. You have to understand that this isn't just about
being scared."

"I do understand that." Dominic rubbed Morgan's fingers.
"Go on."

"The wind had swung onshore." He shut his eyes. "The surf
breaking over the Devil's Anvil's quite something, if the sea and wind
run in a particular combination. I had to go and look."

"I get that. Like having to watch a train wreck."

"Yep. Granddad used to say 'God bless all sailors on a night like
this.' He'd seen ships out there in distress on several occasions, and
he believed it was stupid for people to think they'd tamed the world.
That you couldn't ever tame the sea." The dam had been breached,
words tumbling out over each other. "The night I'm talking about was
in late August. Keep that date in mind. Out at sea, I spotted what I
assumed was a replica sailing ship, one of those sail-training jobs that
usually have a backup engine."

"Ah, yes. To ease them home or out of port when the wind isn't
doing what it's supposed to." Dominic didn't sound like he approved.

"It was a three-masted vessel, a frigate by the shape of it. She
appeared to be authentic, although I knew that nothing from the time

of Trafalgar could still be afloat. I kept telling myself she was either a charity job or a rich man's plaything. The ship was foundering, breaking deep and taking on water. Not only that, she was being driven onto the lee shore by the stiff wind, sure to dash on the rocks."

"Good God."

Neither needed to mention the name *Troilus*; its presence was almost palpable. Same type of ship. Same time of year. "I ran to dial 999, get out the coastguards or something, but the line was dead, and I never considered using my mobile. Or maybe I did and the battery was flat." Funny how the practical bits of what happened seemed less clear in his memory than the mental image of the ship foundering.

"What did your parents do?"

"Nothing. They weren't here. They'd gone to a bank do down in Padstow and were staying over. Eddie was staying at a mate's, so I had the run of the house—I'd thought it was such a treat." He shivered. "I'll grab another blanket. Could be a long session."

Morgan carried on with the story as he tucked them up. How he'd gone back to his bedroom, able to do nothing other than watch helplessly through the window. "The top of something—I guess it was the main mast—went with a crack almost as loud as the thunder. The ship started, I don't know how to describe it, flailing about." He shrugged uncomfortably.

"It sounds horrific." Dominic snuggled closer.

"It was ghastly. I had to go out and see if there was anything I could do. Not sure what I had in mind, but you can't stand by and do nothing. I nearly got swept off my feet by the wind when I got outside, but I'd had the sense to put on waterproofs. I've never known a night like it, before or since."

"You were lucky you didn't go over the cliff. Like you thought I was going to."

"I know. That's the odd thing, though. I didn't feel in any danger, myself." Morgan suddenly realised he had Dominic's hand in his but wasn't sure how it had got there. "That's why it must have simply been a dream, or a hallucination or whatever. No matter how real it felt. At least . . ."

"At least what? You can't leave me dangling there, like a cliff-hanger in a bad TV series."

Morgan managed a laugh. "This is going to sound completely loony. I was awake when I got down to the cliff path—I know it wasn't a dream from the rollicking I got from my mother when she found all my wet clothes the next day. I pretended I'd been out to help a motorist with a flat tyre. I had to tell a hell of a lot of lies."

"I bet she didn't believe any of them. I guess you never told her the truth?"

"God, no. You see, when I got down to the cliff that night, not only had the storm eased off into drizzle, there was no ship. And it wasn't as if she'd just gone down, because there was nothing. No debris, no masts or spars or men in the water." Nothing except a horrible sickening feeling in his stomach. "I went back to the house and looked at the phone. And I knew that if I picked it up, there'd be a dialling tone. Which I did and there was, all working perfectly and no evidence the lines had ever been down, as I found out subsequently. I did quite a bit of research, over the next few days."

"You didn't ring the coastguard? When you found the line working."

"Would you have done? And risk being accused of making nuisance calls, especially if you'd convinced yourself that it had all been a dream? They'd have thought I'd been on the wacky baccy."

"And had you? Or the gin? Come on, home alone and all that . . ."

If Dominic hadn't been grinning, Morgan might have lumped him one. "I'd had nothing worse than strong coffee. And I was clearheaded enough to make sure I scoured the news and the weather and all the rest of it. There'd not been a shipwreck, nor even a storm as bad as I'd witnessed. But there was the story about *Troilus*."

"I didn't want to mention that."

"I guessed the time of year would ring a bell. And the circumstances." It had rung a vague bell at the time. Over the days following the dream, he'd researched the exact date of the wreck, found out that *Troilus*—the beloved *Troilus* so much a part of the fabric of their lives—had been a fifth-rate frigate, like the one he'd seen. Spookily alike, if the old pictures (pictures he might well have seen as a child and had forgotten about) were to be believed. And she'd been blown onto these very rocks—*his* rocks, the ones he saw every day from his room—back in 1794.

"No wonder you've winced when I've banged on about the wreck. And what a pillock I was asking if the bay was haunted." Dominic's face had paled, despite the fire's glow.

"You weren't to know." Nor was he to know that his arrival had brought that long-buried dream right to the surface.

"There'll be a logical reason behind it. The dream. Why you had it in the first place and why it's come back. Although I'd imagine that the strain of the last few days might account for the recurrence."

"True." Morgan certainly felt run ragged.

"Although it's odd." Dominic frowned. "If it was simply a dream, that first time, how did you end up down by the cliff path?"

"Buggered if I know. As far as I'm aware, I have no history of sleepwalking."

"Which suggests you were awake and having a hallucination, or experiencing some distortion of reality. Or else . . ." Dominic stopped. "This is no conversation for the middle of the night."

"You're right. We should try to get a bit of shut-eye and that isn't going to happen if we scare ourselves shitless. No talking about nightmares."

More to the point, no suggesting he'd seen a ghost ship. Or, worse than that, the faint possibility that this wasn't just a nightmare; that Morgan had shown signs of losing his marbles at an earlier age than his mother had.

Maybe his mother had suffered these same worries, been watching for every little sign that she was going the same way as her mother and grandmother; she was an intelligent woman who wouldn't have buried her head in the sand. If so, to have lived with that torment and never once revealed it to her children must have been doubly agonising. He wished he could ask her about it now, receive some reassurance, but that too was denied to him, itself a form of bereavement and loss. If he was sliding down that same hill, then he'd be sliding alone.

"Let the thoughts go." Dominic held him close. "Whatever you're torturing yourself with, there's no bloody point. Let's kip down here; pretend we're having a sleepover or something."

"Sounds good. On all points."

Very good. And easier said than done.

CHAPTER EIGHT

The morning was awkward, albeit not as much as Morgan had anticipated; they'd managed to get a few hours' sleep in and had found things to talk about other than ships or senile parents over breakfast. But there'd been something—a sense of being tongue-tied—hanging in the air between them. Dominic, as he'd left, had deliberately stroked the ballast stone as they'd gone down the path, like a lover's last caress. *They* hadn't even shared a hug, waking on different settees and not really getting any closer all morning.

"Have a safe flight. Ring me when you get home." Morgan smiled brightly as they reached Dominic's car, forcing back his guilt and confusion. He'd *know*, when that call came, whether it would generate longing and desire, or just the hope that Dominic would forget about him and that bloody ship. Maybe the bloke wouldn't ring at all, too disturbed by the revelations of the night before.

"I'll do that. Thanks for taking care of me so well." Dominic fiddled with his car keys, although he seemed reluctant to get going. The "is there going to be another time?" moment had arrived, and neither of them seemed sure how to approach it.

"Are you planning to come back to carry on your research?" That was a safe enough question.

"Planning to, yes. I have to find out more about John Lawson, set things straight. I can use the time in between to work out how and where I'm going to find what I need." Dominic's smile leavened another uncomfortable lump of a pause, although there was still no mention of *Can I treat you to a proper dinner instead of fish and chips?*

"I was . . ." they both said in unison, then laughed, nervously.

"Go on, you first," Morgan said.

"I was going to propose . . ." Dominic's suggestion got nipped in the bud, as Morgan's mobile went off in his pocket. "You answer that—I need to get away. I'll ring later, I promise."

"Yeah." Morgan fished out the phone. "Now get a move on before I lose a client."

Dominic slapped him on the shoulder—maybe that was in lieu of a hug—and got himself into the car just as Morgan went through the whole "Hello, Cadoc Design" routine. Morgan watched through the open door, only half a mind on his customer, as the hire car pulled out onto the road, and his guest disappeared from sight. Would it be safer if that were the last view he ever had of him?

He finished the call, then got to work on his sadly neglected email inbox, trying to ignore the question of what to do about Dominic. The sound of his mobile insistently announcing the arrival of a message got initially ignored, Morgan habitually avoiding reading texts while he was working, but once bitten was twice shy. He checked the message. Nothing to do with his mum, this time, but the other problem. Dominic. The bloke must have got his phone out to text almost as soon as he'd arrived at the terminal building.

Dominic: *Didn't finish my sentence earlier. Wanted to offer to buy you a proper meal next time. Still owe you. Don't feel you have to say yes. I'll be down here anyway, chasing midshipmen. Dom.*

The words leaped off the screen and into Morgan's ears, in Dominic's distinctive, shy tones. He hadn't the heart to turn the bloke down.

Morgan: *Sounds good to me. What about the next bank holiday?* His fingers hovered over the keys, then seemed to take on a life, and mind, of their own. *There's always room for you at the house. Don't feel obliged to take up the offer.* Bloody English reserve—were they always going to be pussyfooting around things? He got his head down over his inbox before any answer could come, ignoring the inevitable text tone until he had dealt with some more of his incoming post.

Dominic: *Late May might work. Have to check no parental three-line whip on for that weekend. Would love to stay again, if that's okay. Do say if you have second thoughts. I'd understand. Don't want to cause any more nightmares. Dom. X.*

The sudden appearance of the kiss made Morgan smile. What a pair of pillocks they were. He decided to read the second message before replying to the first.

Dominic: *You can't tell me off in person for saying sorry so . . . sorry if I flushed out elephants again. Won't mention the dreams if you don't want me to. Dom. X.*

There were the get-out clauses, if he needed them. Dominic seemed content to come back here and play at finding two-hundred-year-old midshipmen, while sharing the benefits of a double bed. Or not, if that's how things panned out. If he was worrying that Morgan was losing his marbles or agonising over the fact that their falling into bed was a mistake, he wasn't showing it.

Morgan stared out of the window, unseeing.

"Do you want to go out with him?" Well, that, to coin a phrase, was the question.

He liked Dominic, liked him a lot. The bloke was good company and sympathetic, so what wasn't to like? Last night had been cracking in the bed department, and cathartic in the heart-to-heart section. So why had they been so bloody awkward with each other this morning and why was the thought of seeing him the next bank holiday tinged with a pint or two of dread?

Morgan left it as long as was decent before answering—about two cups of coffee and a batch of washing—and then he kept his answer light and noncommittal.

Morgan: *Sorry for delay in reply. Was being domestic. Let me know when you have arrangements for the bank holiday sorted. Speak soon.*

That would have to do until he got his head screwed on right. Any hopes that maybe Dominic would stall on his answer were soon blown out of the water.

Dominic: *Will do. Just landed. Now for the fun and games with the baggage carousel. Have had some ideas about getting gen on Lawson. I'll expand anon.*

Morgan groaned. Was this the way the next three weeks would go, texts flying the breadth of England every five minutes? That's how it had been with James, the first few days, but this didn't feel like those mad early stages of a fledgling romance; it felt as though they'd actually known each other for years and somehow the first signs of autumn frost had tinged their relationship's blossoms.

The pragmatic approach would be to defer his replies, be friendly but not "in your face," keeping things simmering but strictly on the back burner, then wait to see if the great healer—time—would also bring a dose of wisdom.

It didn't, at least in the short term. Dominic's phone call came three days later, with apologies, naturally, for the delay in getting in touch. Yes, he was free of commitments for the bank holiday, no his family didn't mind him jetting off again.

"To be honest, my mother seems pleased I've got myself . . ." there was a short, telling pause, "a sympathetic ear for the ship stuff."

"Look . . . Dominic . . ." Morgan hated talking over the phone—there was something about not seeing the other person's eyes which meant you could never really get across what you were trying to say. Almost as bad as exchanging texts.

"You don't have to say anything. It's all right. I mean, if you only want us to be friends." He sounded like he was disappointed but trying to put on a brave face. That was horribly poignant.

"Truth is, I'm confused, mate. Monday night was great, all of it, even the dreams. You're the first person I've been able to talk to about them. You have no idea how good that made me feel."

"It made me feel good too." There was a pause, as though Dominic was weighing up how much of his heart to heave into his mouth. "Is this about Tuesday morning?"

Morgan gasped, which must have echoed down the phone. "I've always said you were a mind reader. Yes, it is. Where did the big dose of awkward come from?"

"Ah. That would be me, I think. Sorry."

"You're banned from using that word, remember?"

"Well, how *am* I to apologise, then? I've been worrying I've made the situation difficult for you. You were at a low ebb, because of the dreams and everything, and I've a feeling I forced your arm. Don't often get any really nice guys responding to me and I took my chance."

Dominic's sigh rattled the phone. "If your confusion means you've had second thoughts about wanting to be involved with me, tell me now and put me out of my misery. I can handle us being friends."

"You didn't force me to do anything I didn't want to do. I was worried things were the other way round. Or something." That *something* would have to cover all the other whirling thoughts. "Keep in touch, eh? And then, when you come down here, we'll see how we feel."

"That works for me. As long as you remember I'm not good with relationships. Don't particularly understand what I have to do."

"Just be yourself."

While they were at it, maybe Morgan could work out what being *himself* meant. And if that involved a descent like his mother had endured.

CHAPTER NINE

I f time was going to bring wisdom, it needed to get its skates on.
Dominic kept in touch, not too eagerly, and didn't chance his
arm. He said he'd taken an option on a hotel for the days after the
bank holiday, so he could progress his research without imposing
on Morgan's hospitality, an arrangement which suited them both. If
things took a turn for the better, the hotel could be cancelled.

Morgan still couldn't decide whether the fling with Dominic had
been a good idea or one of his worst. Irrespective of the challenges a
long-distance relationship might present, the long term was an issue
too. He didn't want to lumber anybody with taking care of him the
way he'd had to take care of his mother. James would have legged it at
the first sign of illness—perhaps that was what he'd already done—but
Dominic was too nice a guy to do that.

Their reunion took place early on the Friday evening of the
bank holiday weekend, Dominic having, literally, got a flyer. He'd
rocked up to the door of Cadoc while Morgan was dealing with a
local client who'd dropped in unexpectedly to arrange a contract
extension. Morgan apologised, asked Dominic to make a cup of
tea—and make himself at home—and by the time the lucrative
customer transaction had been completed, the potential for
awkwardness had dissipated. His guest was ensconced at the kitchen
table, looking every inch like he belonged there. Morgan couldn't
take that as a sign.

"Thanks for putting up with me again. I've brought a thank-you
present." Dominic picked up his backpack, then rummaged in it.

"You didn't need to, although—" Morgan stopped, gingerly
accepting the object he was given. "Um, what *is* this?"

"It's an old toy cannon. Ship's one, as you can tell from the gun carriage." Dominic's eyes danced. "I saw it in the market and thought of you. It's real copper. Used to fire little cartridges or something, once. In the days before health and safety ruled the world."

"It's lovely." Morgan meant it. An exquisite item, shined up, surely, by Dominic's own hands. "I'm not sure 'thank you' from me says enough."

"Would it ease your conscience if I said it was far less expensive than a hotel room for the weekend?" Dominic suddenly seemed to find his hands the most interesting thing in the world. "I put my bags in the spare room. I didn't want to presume."

"Come on." Morgan stood, offering his guest his hand. "What will be cracking at the moment is a trip down to the cove. Before the light goes. If you fancy it?"

Dominic grabbed Morgan's hand and leaped up. "What do you think?"

As they headed for the cliff path, Morgan tried to order his thoughts; Dominic's bag in the guest room now, Dominic in *his* bed last time, that little cannon presented to him so tenderly. None of it was helping get his mind straight.

"I haven't had that dream again," he ventured. "Not since the night you were here."

"That's good. I didn't want to ask, in case it turned out I'd been the one who'd caused the recurrence." Dominic studied the road. "It seemed like it was."

"No, it wasn't you. Honest." Morgan was suddenly sure of that, although he couldn't say why. "I was getting recurrences before I first met you." They'd all coincided with emotional turmoil, of course. Dad's death, Mum going into the home, first signs of James cooling off.

"You're remarkably chipper about it."

"Compared to last time? Yeah, well it's easier to be chipper on a sunny evening than in the middle of the night. Anyway, I've built up coping mechanisms." Morgan ran his hands through his hair, thinking of all the occasions he'd had to learn to muddle through. "Used to be that if the sea got up and the wind was blowing from the north, I kept the curtains shut until it had blown through. Changed my bedroom as soon as I could. It all helped."

"Come on, let's chase all the bad thoughts away!" Dominic broke into a trot, tugging Morgan along with him.

"Steady on, you'll come a crop—" Morgan grabbed at Dominic's arm, just as his foot caught in a rabbit scrape and sent him flying. "I said you were a bloody idiot. I was right."

Dominic sprang back onto his feet, dusting off his trousers. "It was only a trip."

"A trip? You could have slipped on the wet grass and gone over the sodding edge." Morgan remembered taking a tumble down the cliff path, when he was barely out of short trousers. He'd got away with it lightly, nothing worse than a sprain and a mass of scrapes and bruises, but his mother had flayed him with her tongue when he'd expected sympathy and relief. At last he understood why she'd been so cross.

"I'm all right. Only got a few scratches."

"Because I caught you. You could have broken your fucking neck. Maybe you should have done, to teach you a lesson."

Dominic turned pale, much paler than he'd been as he'd been hauled up from the cliff edge. "You don't mean that. Please say you don't."

Morgan took a deep breath, the sudden, totally incongruous need to laugh sweeping over him. Was it relief? The fact that Dominic looked so scared? Whatever the reason, he wouldn't give the bloke— or his own conflicting emotions—the satisfaction of lightening the moment. "No, I don't. Sorry. That was the shock talking. But I do wish you'd grow a brain. You really could have got yourself killed."

"You don't need to tell me that." Dominic's wide-eyed fright had turned into a grimace. "The twinge in my back's making it plain."

Oh hell. Another bank-holiday dash to the hospital? "I'll call an ambulance. Can you move everything?"

"Yes, I can. And no, there's nothing broken, so don't call anybody. I'm fine."

Morgan drew breath. Dominic didn't deserve a tongue-lashing simply because he was clumsy. Or was *he* overreacting because of the falls his mother had suffered? Back there again.

"You'd better have a rest anyway, just in case." He led them, almost unspeaking, up to the house and through to the lounge, awakening memories of that night spent in front of the fire.

Dominic eyed the settee, warily. "Should I go? I always seem to make you angry."

"No, it's not you, it's me. I shouldn't have got so arsy."

"You were. I know I could have hurt myself, but you were out of order."

"I said I was sorry." Morgan drew his hand across his forehead. "I seem to get arsy all the time, now."

"Maybe you should have a word with the doctor." Dominic eased himself onto the sofa. "See whether it's to do with your celestial action replays."

"My what?"

"Your recurring nightmares."

"Do you really think that's what are? Some sort of rip in the continuity of space and time that's giving me a window into the past?" Morgan strode across the room to where he could gaze out into the garden; he didn't want to risk another argument. "Maybe I'm just going loopy."

"You don't believe that any more than I do."

"Don't I?" Morgan shrugged. "Aren't the family genes coming out? I'm already forgetful—I couldn't recall who Lawson was, remember?"

"That was probably stress. Don't be so hard on yourself."

"Hmm. Be that as it may, I wish I knew what the dreams were about." Morgan hadn't wanted to discuss the nightmares, but here they were, making themselves felt again.

"Don't ask me. I'm all theories and no concrete answers." Dominic, wincing, slipped a pillow into the small of his back. "Like this pulled muscle, your dreams will have a simple explanation."

Morgan snorted. "Will they? I suppose it'll be stress-induced delirium, or hallucinations. Sleepwalking, haunting. I'm sorry, but they feel way too scary to analyse too closely."

Dominic stroked the arm of the settee. "When I was here before, you had a nightmare. You didn't go wandering or sleepwalking or anything similar. Not that time."

"I know. It's odd. I only ever went wandering the once. That first time." Morgan dropped into a chair. "Since then, when the dreams come back, I relive the whole thing. Dream within the dream, the phone not working, leaving the house, the sudden blast of cold air on my cheek when I reach the cliff edge."

"Do you dream you're shouting? You made a hell of a noise."

"Yes, I suppose I do. I wouldn't know." And that was another awful thing to impose on a lover. Disturbed nights for all the wrong reasons.

"Recurring dreams aren't that uncommon."

"Recurring dreams of an event I couldn't have witnessed but seem to have an accurate knowledge of? Because that's the truly scary bit, isn't it?"

"Maybe your brain simply churns out a storyline based on what you heard as a child, so young that you've no conscious memory of it. Your family must have discussed the wreck." Dominic—so nice, so trusting—didn't he deserve better? "Elements of that account that got locked away deep in the cerebral vaults, as much a part of your memory as the beams are part of your house. Until something freed them."

That made a bit of sense. Morgan's great-grandmother had died when he was only four, and it was exactly the sort of tale the old lady would have recounted to him as he sat on her knee. "But what could have prompted it to break free from the vaults? And in such a dramatic fashion?"

"Like I suggested earlier: stress, perhaps. About twice a year it's manic at work and I find myself so frazzled I end up doing weird things. Even weirder than normal, before you make any smart-alec remarks."

Morgan couldn't help but laugh. "Not a word was going to cross my lips. I don't think I was that stressed when I was a teenager, though. And if this is all about stories I heard at my great-gran's knee, why are the dreams so vivid? And don't give me any reincarnation-theory crap. I don't believe I was a little lad on the shore two hundred odd years ago."

"Reincarnation? Who mentioned that? Has someone given you that crap already?" Dominic frowned.

"No. Yes. Bugger." Morgan exhaled, loudly. "It's not exactly true that I've never talked about these dreams before. Just not to anybody who mattered." He rushed on, before Dominic spotted *mattered*. "I got drunk one night in a bar in London and poured my heart out to this random bloke. Exposed my soul, although that was all I exposed."

"Glad to hear it. Strange blokes in London bars! You could have ended up having your kidneys sold."

Morgan sniggered. Trust Dominic to make exactly the right joke and steer them through such a difficult passage. "That's too near the truth to be funny. It was a damn close run thing with that particular guy; someone else picked him up two nights later and ended up wallet-less and bruised like an overripe banana."

Dominic screwed his face up. "Nasty. We've all been there, done that though, on the hunt for sympathy when we've been rat-arsed."

Morgan wasn't sure Dominic had ever done any such thing, but it was nice of him to pretend. "Anyway, this nasty piece of work told me I must have seen the wreck of *Troilus* from the cliffs, in a former life. And I was going through a process of reliving it, taking myself back to the original place."

"As a theory, it has no scientific merit. Although maybe there's a strange element of truth there. Not you in some former life, but a previous member of the Capell family could have stood on that cliff and witnessed the wreck. Then later on, he or she would have told their daughter, or their sons, or whatever. Handing the story down, father or mother to child until it reached you." Dominic's eyes shone. "Like the story of the beams and the boulder. Equally grounded in truth."

"The beams don't scare the crap out of me. Or give me nightmares." Morgan stared at the unlit fire; it suddenly felt like some idiot had gone and dropped the air temperature ten degrees.

"So have you *ever* talked to a doctor about it?"

"Have I hell." Morgan snorted. He'd probably not seen a doctor since he was a boy, with pneumonia. "I'm not ill." Maybe if he kept telling himself that, he'd believe it.

Dominic frowned. "Better somebody who knows what they're talking about than a guy in a bar. You need to get those dreams out in the open where you can examine them and see they're nothing to be frightened of."

"Right." Morgan smiled, despite his uneasiness. Dominic and his wonderfully pragmatic and logical approach to any problem.

"A problem shared is a problem halved. Perhaps you could describe all of what you saw in your dream. If I could pick out any substantial mistakes, then that might prove it must have been based on childhood tales. A real ghostly manifestation wouldn't get the details wrong. Like stigmata. If they really were the marks of Jesus's crucifixion, wouldn't the nail imprints be on the wrists?"

"I have no bloody idea. If you say so." It made sense, though. Everything Dominic said seemed to be making sense at present. "But what if history's got the details wrong, like artists have done with the pictures of the crucifixion and the painters in the museum did with the wreck? We wouldn't be able to tell, then."

"Don't complicate matters unnecessarily." Dominic jabbed at him with his hand. "Maybe it's not such a good idea, anyway. If it turns out you're spot on, with the level of detail you couldn't have known unless you'd researched the wreck as much as I've done, which you obviously haven't . . ."

"If? Yes? If it turns out I'm right, then what?"

"Then we're liable to scare the pants off you. Not that I don't like you with your pants off, but I'd rather find another way of doing it."

"Daft sod." Morgan shut his eyes, took another deep breath. "I refuse to discuss those dreams any further. Not here, not now, but thank you."

"My pleasure. Except what have I done to be thanked for?"

"Cheered me up. Talked sense. Made the unbearable bearable." Morgan leaned over, just able to reach Dominic's hand as it lay on the arm rest. Making a romantic overture seemed wrong, given all his worries about dragging a good bloke into sharing his mess of a life, but he needed the comfort. "Everything seems so ordinary when you're around."

Dominic flushed. "While we're talking old family stories, you don't happen to remember any relating to John Lawson? Nothing lurking about the dank recesses of memory?"

"If I had, I'd have said. Unless they're buried so deep I need a hypnotist to unlock them. No," Morgan shook his head, "I didn't volunteer for the experiment. And anyway, wouldn't that be a ridiculous coincidence?"

"A bigger coincidence than you having the *Troilus* beams in your house? That ship's woven into the fabric of your family history, isn't it?" Dominic patted Morgan's hand. "I'm glad I came back. Not simply to run John Lawson to ground."

"I'm pleased you came back, as well." Morgan smiled. They sat in silence for a while, as the light outside the window ebbed, until a growl erupted from Dominic's stomach. "I want my dinner; my stomach's grumbling away like mad."

"And there was me thinking it was thunder. I—" Morgan stopped as Dominic's mobile rang.

My mother, Dominic mouthed, on answering. Morgan watched and listened while Dominic explained that he *had* remembered his aunt's birthday, that a card and present had been sent, and that he'd definitely make the big family do in June. He'd glanced across at the mention of that, so Morgan had shrugged and turned away, suddenly envious at the fond intimacy on show. He'd never again be able to talk to Mum like that, unless they both ended up gaga and found they understood each other again.

Why the hell couldn't Morgan summon up the courage to find out once and for all what was going on with him? Was it only because he was scared the medical opinion would be that he was indeed going mad? Or was he worried they'd say he was fine and he'd have to find the real reason he was in such a state?

Dinner turned out to be a success. They'd gone nowhere fancier than the local pub, but that was a place which could turn out a rare seafood platter, most of it locally caught. Morgan had felt too lazy to walk, and so his guest's pulled muscle gave a ready-made excuse to take the car. Dominic had insisted on both driving and paying, saying that he'd also be the one to take one for the team and avoid alcohol; they had to safely negotiate the potentially treacherous lanes in the dark.

Once they were home, they hit both the sauvignon blanc and the sofa.

"Our last family holiday here was when I was eighteen," Dominic remarked, out of the blue and halfway through his first glass of wine. "I vowed I'd come back on my own—which I did—but it's never the same, is it?"

"Nope." Morgan sipped his wine. It would be very easy to say, *Would you think about doing a re-run of your childhood holidays? What about having a week here in the summer?* but that would be committing both of them. He had to remember how he'd felt that early May Tuesday morning, how confusing it had all been. How confusing it still was.

"Maybe this week will feel like it used to. I've got a focus now. Lawson, I mean," Dominic added, hurriedly. "I'm not assuming you'll be at my beck and call the next few days."

Morgan smiled. "I knew that. You're okay." He took another drink. "Can I ask a really personal question?"

"As long as I don't have to guarantee I'll answer," Dominic replied, in an unnaturally airy way. They were back to walking on eggshells.

"You don't need to answer. You can punch me in the jaw if you like. It's just that you've not mentioned any boyfriends. I wanted to be clear in my mind." Was that too close, to *me and you and what sort of relationship we have—or haven't*?

"No punch required," Dominic said, before draining his glass, then reaching for the bottle to refill it. "There's nobody pining at home who thinks I spent my last visit here solely on ship's business."

"That's good. It's good that I've not queered anyone's pitch." Why wouldn't Morgan's mouth behave itself?

"You haven't. I admit I've had my moments, some really good ones. But the guys who tend to hang around aren't all that great, and nice guys don't seem to want to stay." Dominic rolled his eyes. "Oh God, I sound a total snivelling idiot. I'm not trying to talk myself back into your bed by making you feel sorry for me. And I know long-distance relationships are hard work."

"Yeah, they are. And I know you're not. After years of putting up with James, I appreciate your honesty, believe me." Morgan topped up his own glass.

"Well, if I've got free rein to be honest, I've got to tell you that what happened last time was brilliant. At the risk of still sounding like a loser, I have to say that blokes like you don't usually look twice at blokes like me. Too many other tempting cakes at the Waitrose bakery counter."

"I bet they'd look twice if you smiled more often." Morgan stroked his arm. "Your whole face changes when you smile."

"That's what I've been doing wrong, then," Dominic replied, grinning.

"See? You're material for Rugby's Finest now."

"Sorry?"

"It's a calendar. Like Dieux du Stade. Well, a bit like it—fewer naked backsides." Morgan was gabbling again. Flirting. Doing all the things he'd had no intention of doing; that grin of Dominic's had hit him straight below the belt line.

"Nope." Dominic shrugged. "No idea what you're talking about. I'll take it as a compliment, though."

"You do that. And search for those calendars up on Google sometime, only not at work." Morgan smirked. "You're a disgrace to the gay community, not knowing about all that eye candy."

"I should be taken onto the parade ground and have my copy of *Priscilla, Queen of the Desert* ripped from me." *That* smile again.

Morgan took a deep breath. They'd reached a watershed, the conversation and the exchange of glances well into the field of flirtation exactly as they'd been in the car with the fish and chips. If he made a move, Dominic was bound to respond; if he didn't make a move, would the bloke understand? He opted for the coward's way. "I'll be back in a mo. Need a slash."

It had to be done, and not simply to ease his bladder. Relieving himself, his thoughts whirred around his brain.

Why shouldn't he get into bed with Dominic again? He was a genuinely decent bloke, good in the sack, good to be around, somebody with whom Morgan didn't have to put on any pretences or put up any barriers. He knew about the dreams—and the Capell family problems—and he was still here. And he'd probably be here for as long as Morgan wanted him to be.

So what was really the problem? The obvious difficulties of a long-distance relationship, or not wanting to lumber Dominic with a boyfriend who might need a carer a couple of years down the line?

Finish off. Zip trousers. Wash hands. Stare into the mirror. Give self a talking to about overthinking things. Keep overthinking them.

When Morgan got back to the lounge, Dominic appeared to be lost in thought.

"Penny for them?" Morgan asked, which was always a risky question.

"They're overpriced at a penny," Dominic replied. "I was wishing I'd not been such a wimp over dinner. Should have had that apple pudding."

"Is that all?" Morgan hoped he didn't sound too relieved. "That's soon sorted. Want to go and raid the kitchen?"

He grabbed his guest's hand and gently pulled him up. If they *did* share a bed tonight, against all Morgan's better judgement, he'd have to be careful the bloke didn't pull that muscle again. They also needed to walk up those stairs sober, knowing exactly the decision they'd made; dessert would help soak up the alcohol too. In the end, while they couldn't match apple pudding, they put together a decent plateful—toast, jam, strawberries, and some nice chocolate—and took it back to the lounge.

"That was cracking," Dominic said, when they'd had their fill. Then he smiled, which was fatal for Morgan. Good wine, comfort food, *that* smile, all the things which had been brewing had bubbled up, and no amount of talking to himself in the mirror was going to keep the lid on them.

He reached over and straightened Dominic's collar. "This has gone all skew whiff."

"My collars never behave." Dominic fiddled with it himself, his lack of the expected reaction frustrating. Morgan's earlier thought that he wouldn't be fussed if they didn't have sex was rapidly becoming irrelevant.

"I met a friend of your ex last week, although *friend* might be breaking the Trades Descriptions Act."

"Oh." Where was this going?

"He told me James was a right bastard."

"He was." Morgan wished James wouldn't keep reappearing, like a spectre at the feast. He had enough apparitions to get his head around. "Water under the bridge."

"Like the water you drink abroad and end up with Montezuma's revenge." Dominic laughed, grabbing Morgan's hand and bringing it up to his face. "Anyway, you deserve somebody who'll treat you with honesty and decency."

Morgan hadn't misread the situation, then; it sounded like Dominic was applying for the job. Shame it might not be a permanent appointment.

"Blokes like that don't grow on trees." Morgan leaned closer, taking the next step in the complex dance they'd seemed to have decided, without conscious agreement, to embark on. "In the meantime, would you compromise?"

"Compromise?" Dominic's voice had grown huskier, rich velvet tones emerging, as they had last time, up in Morgan's bed.

"I can't promise that I'm perfect, because I know I'm not. And I can't promise you anything, really. I'm too confused about what's going on in my head for a start. But I like you a lot, and if you don't mind me vacillating, we—" The state-of-Morgan's-nation speech got cut off with a kiss.

"Don't sell yourself short," Dominic said, once they came up for air. "And please don't say anything you're going to regret later. I've ordered myself not to fall for you hook, line, and sinker." He produced yet another devastating smile. "So long as we can stay friends of some sort, I'm happy. And if it's one in the eye . . ." He stopped, smiling sheepishly.

"One in the eye for who?" Morgan could guess, but it would be fun to hear Dominic say it.

"For James. Is it a problem that I get a kick thinking I'm here with you and he was too blind to see what a great bloke you are?"

"Not at all," Morgan almost purred, until his catlike contentment was suddenly broken by a horrible thought. "Did he try anything on with you? Kind of thing he does."

"What, pick up lost waifs like me? Good grief no. He had his eye on this Old-Etonian rugby-player type he had tagging along. I guess that's why he was spouting the historical stuff. Trying to impress him with his vast knowledge."

No wonder James had been so keen to make it plain that the Cornwall connection had been severed. And maybe the Old Etonian had been about to be given the obligatory "You might just be Mr. Right" speech. Fat lot of good it would do him.

"Let's not talk about James. He'll put a total damper on the evening." Morgan pulled Dominic close for another kiss, a long, lingering one this time. Forgetting about James took precedence for the moment over any other worries. "You do this bit better than he ever did, anyway."

"Do I? Well, there's a turn up." Dominic returned another kiss, which couldn't have been easy when Morgan had started to chuckle. "What's so funny?"

"You." Morgan stroked Dominic's cheek.

"I suppose I am. And you're not much better." Dominic drew the fingers to his mouth. "When I first spoke to you over the phone, I thought you had a poker up your backside. All that stuff about 'your first task is to find my address' and the rest of the crap. That was like a red rag to a bull. I hate being told I can't do something. It made me twice as determined to get in touch."

Morgan groaned. "Was I that up myself? You'll have to forgive me. I'd only that morning received the 'Dear Morgan' letter from the bloody rat who doesn't deserve his name used."

Dominic slipped his hand round the back of Morgan's head, caressing his hair. "I like 'Bloody Rat.' That suits him down to the ground. Or to his rat hole."

"Nice one." Time to forget James, no matter how much he kept wanting to be remembered. Time to cut the words and get into action. "Come on." Morgan didn't want to do it here, on what had been his parents' sofa, in full view of the family portrait on the wall. He eased himself out of his seat, stopping himself grabbing Dominic's hand again to pull him up. "I've got a nice bed upstairs. Trouble is it's too big and too empty."

"Is that a clumsy way of asking me if I'd like to fill it? Oh, do grow up." Dominic grinned at Morgan's laughter. "Must you find the smut in everything? It's like being in an episode of *Round the Horne*."

"Nothing wrong with that. The repeats were favourite listening in our house."

Dominic's grin widened. "I never understood the jokes, not until I was in my teens. They got away with filth."

"Of course they did. Innocent days, nobody got the slang. The average little old lady listening as she washed up the Sunday-lunch things wasn't going to get the significance of a cottage upright."

"Talking of which . . ." Dominic's hand swept against something which was pretty well upright beneath Morgan's trousers.

"Come on." Morgan took Dominic's hand, edging him towards the door. "We've talked too long."

Dominic wound his arms around Morgan's waist, pulling him close for another kiss. Morgan enjoyed the sensation of his tongue's explorations, savouring the sensation when his fingers started exploring the small of Morgan's back. They progressed towards the door, snogging as they walked backwards in some strange, crablike variation on ballroom dancing that needed mouths as well as arms and legs.

When they reached the stairs, Morgan broke the clinch. "We'll never get upstairs in one piece if we try to like this."

"Spoilsport."

"Don't blame me—blame gravity." As soon as they hit the top stair, they went back into the walking hug, Morgan relieved that he'd had the foresight to change his sheets, so the duvet cover, as they rolled onto it, felt smooth and cool. Time to keep it simple: soft and slow and sensual.

Dominic tugged gently at Morgan's shirt. "This needs to come off. It *all* needs to come off."

The view from the window, lights twinkling up the headland, was usually enchanting, but it was wasted on them. Dominic had slipped his hand inside Morgan's boxer shorts, so even the *Mona Lisa*, lit up with Christmas lights and dancing the hokey-cokey, would have been wasted on them.

"Ease up—there's no hurry."

"That's not what *this* is telling me." Dominic's hand played havoc down below, having found its target and showing no signs of deceleration. "Does it really have to be 'Frankie says Relax'?"

"Frankie can go to hell," Morgan said, giving in.

Despite all Morgan's misgivings, it was as good as before, and when Dominic came, eyes open wide and looking more ecstatic than Morgan had ever seen him—happier than when he'd been head down over his research, which was saying something—it was the icing on a pretty considerable cake.

"I feel like I want to say thank you," Dominic said, much later, as he caressed Morgan's head in the postcoital glow.

"For what?" Morgan stroked Dominic's chest. Smooth skin, sweet smell of some classy cologne; the bloke got better and better.

"For giving me a second chance. It felt like we'd made a mess of things somehow, last time. Got into a right state the morning after."

"We had. I had." Maybe they were still in a bit of a state. But if he was building Dominic up for a fall at some point, he wasn't going to worry over that now. "Don't let's dwell on it."

"Okay."

"I have a proposal for tomorrow." Morgan felt the need to be generous. Maybe it was that after-sex glow talking, or wanting to compensate Dominic in advance for whatever crap he was bound to drop on him later. "I need to go and visit Mum. You could come with me. Say if you think it's a bloody awful idea."

"I hate to disappoint you, but I think it's a great idea." Dominic smiled, eagerly. "It sounds phony to say 'been there, done that' but I have, with my grandmother. I'm under no illusions; I know what to expect. I can't imagine what it would be like always having to make that trip by yourself."

"Why do you have to be so bloody reasonable?" Morgan sighed, in contented bewilderment. "Promise I don't have to pretend I'm brave or that things are okay when they aren't?"

"Do you really think you have to pretend anything with me?"

Pointless to reply: they both knew the answer.

"Curl up in here tonight, if you want." The guest bedroom seemed a long way away and Morgan's bed was going to feel empty without Dominic in it.

"Sounds good to me. Have to use the facilities. Sorry to be so unromantic."

"You bloody well said sorry again." Morgan punched his lover's arm. "I'm going to thump you every time from now on."

"Not fair! I was brought up to be polite."

"Then you better learn to be rude or you'll be black and blue." Morgan snuggled down again, trying not to think of the mess of food and crockery downstairs that needed tidying away or entertain guilty thoughts about boring matters like not having cleaned his teeth. Or important things like his mental well-being. He wanted to stay nestled here until morning, in a dreamless sleep, with no decisions to make and nothing emotional to mull over. It had been too long since life had felt uncomplicated.

CHAPTER TEN

The next morning didn't prove as awkward as their first morning after had.

They'd found themselves comfy in each other's arms, excited enough for a brief early-hours bout of what had gone on the night before. Dominic's muscles had shown no after-effects from his slip, so the cautious edge to their lovemaking could be discarded.

Later, they'd shared the typical small talk that new lovers did, got up to make a pot of tea and a pile of toast, then taken it into the garden, wrapping themselves in blankets against the slight nip in the air. Dominic even managed to get through to draining the last dreg and scooping up the last crumb without once using the word *sorry*, despite the fact he'd nearly sent the teapot flying.

"Are you sure you want me to come with you this morning? I could make myself scarce if you're having second thoughts." Dominic stroked Morgan's arm. "I wouldn't be offended."

"I know you wouldn't. And I haven't changed my mind. It'll do Mum good to see somebody different, and she might remember something about the beams. It happens—some little gem of a fact gets dragged up from the vaults."

"Fingers crossed for that, then." Dominic kept his hand on Morgan's arm, smoothing the skin. "Do you mind clarifying a couple of things for me?"

"Go ahead."

"I'm sorry to ask, but I'm just trying to understand things better. About your mum."

"Go on." Morgan mentally braced himself.

"With Gran, the change came suddenly. Fine one week, next week on the slippery slope. Were there any early warning signs with your mum?"

Morgan should have expected a question like that, but it still felt like a slap to the face. "Are you suggesting I should be keeping an eye out for the same things in me?"

Dominic flinched. "Hey, don't overreact. I did *not* mean that—what kind of a bloke do you think I am?"

"Mea culpa." Morgan rubbed Dominic's hand, trying to recapture the carefree emotions he'd felt earlier, before the reminder that all wasn't well. "I try to be grown-up about the situation, but everything's mixed up in my head."

"And you think I'm not aware of that fact?" Dominic sighed. "My trying to help doesn't seem to be working. Ignore the question."

"No, I'd rather answer. The memory loss came on pretty quickly, like with your gran. There was a family history of it—my grandmother, and her mother before her—although I think we'd swept the whole business under the carpet. Blamed it on one thing or another and never on what it really was. Afterwards, when I thought it through, I wondered if we should have been on the lookout, and caught it as early as we could. There *were* signs, with hindsight, or at least there might have been."

Dominic took Morgan's chin and turned his face towards him. "The only bloody use of hindsight is learning from it. This situation isn't going to repeat itself with any other family member, so you can't. And if you're feeling guilty because you didn't get help for your mum, that's no good, either. Even if you had spotted something, what could you have done, apart from throw everyone into a panic? We all have forgetful moments, we all do daft stuff and it doesn't mean we're losing our marbles. Overanalyse stuff and we'd all be shit scared that we're on the slippery slope. How many times do I have to tell you that?"

"Yes, doctor." Morgan rubbed his cheek on Dominic's arm. "I like you. You're such a beacon of sense in a fog of stupidity."

"You're *not* stupid. You've had a lot on your plate. It'll be all right."

They stayed there, letting the sun kiss their faces until Morgan could put off the inevitable no longer. "We need to get ready. It's open visiting times at the weekend, so best to get my duty done, then we can enjoy the rest of the day."

Dominic leaned in to kiss him. "You're a good bloke, you know. Stop beating yourself up about everything."

That was easier said than done.

The single part of Cornwall Morgan liked least would always be the drive from his house to the nursing home car park, and he'd never enjoyed forcing himself to leave the car and brave what was to come. He'd anticipated it would prove harder with Dominic in tow, but something about the guy's presence was surprisingly calming. A living and breathing dose of tranquilisers.

As Morgan took the keys from the ignition, Dominic touched his arm, and said, "Last time I'll ask this. Are you sure you want me here? Speak now or forever hold your peace."

"Too right I do. I've had to face this alone too often." A couple of times he'd gone with his brother until they'd decided—by mutual but unspoken consent—that it was too difficult, trying to juggle their own emotions and Mum's and not snap at each other. She'd seemed to find it harder having them both there too. Please God she reacted well to Dominic.

"If at any time you want me to leave you two alone, then . . . mention Milton Keynes. I'll say I have to get something from the car, and I'll hang around out here for you."

"That puts a whole new slant on having a safeword." Morgan smiled, tension easing. "I really do appreciate this."

"I won't say it's my pleasure. But I've been in similar places, as you know. It's not easy."

"That's the understatement of the year. And we might be all right, if we catch her at the right time. There'll be a whole ten minutes when you wouldn't think anything was wrong. Sharp as a pin. And then all of a sudden she'll say or do something, and you realise how helpless and vulnerable she is." Morgan reached into the back for the bouquet he'd brought, took a deep breath, and opened the door.

Dominic leaned against the car while Morgan locked it. "Childhood memories are the clearest for your mum, I suppose?"

"Usually. As if they're the most securely embedded, or perhaps the easiest to access. I don't understand why—I'm not sure anyone does." He'd read up about it, talked to the doctors, but it felt like picking at the edges of comprehension. "Come on. I shouldn't dawdle here."

"Yep. You'll feel better if we take the fence at speed."

"You're right." Morgan stared at the nursing home, felt his arm being taken again, and so was across the gravel and in through the door before he could have second thoughts. Sign in at the desk, say hello to the staff, get through the security doors, walk along the corridor, go up in the lift, walk into the day room—it all felt easier on this occasion.

His mother was sitting in the sunshine, knitting needles and wool at hand but not being employed. Time was she'd been a great knitter, and Christine, the nursing sister, was always encouraging her to take it up once more.

"Hello, love." She favoured him with a bright smile as he touched her shoulder. "Ooh, how nice." She reached out with evident pleasure for the bouquet he offered. "They smell beautiful. I've always had a soft spot for freesias." The beam took in Dominic. "Is this your friend?"

"It is. Dominic, this is Mum."

"Pleased to meet you." Dominic extended a hand, as though this were any other meeting.

"Lovely manners." She shook his hand, enthusiastically. "Are the freesias your choice? Young Morgan's not the best judge of flowers."

"They were, but it was a lucky guess."

"Then you'm got excellent taste." As she spoke, the more the true Cornwall accent and dialect—never very noticeable to Morgan's ears—came through. "Are you down here on holiday or is it business?"

"Dominic came to see the roof timbers," Morgan cut in, amused at his mother fixing on the newcomer. She'd always had a soft spot for nice young men.

"The timbers from *Troilus*?" she asked, brightly.

"Ye-es." Morgan had not expected such lucidity. "He's doing some research into the ship's officers. There's one midshipman in particular that interests you, isn't there?"

"Yes." Dominic nodded. "His name was John Lawson. I don't suppose the name rings a bell?"

"Little John Lawson? Oh, everybody knows about him." She turned to Morgan. "Don't you remember?"

"I don't, Mum. Sorry to be so thick. Can you remind me?"

She glanced at Dominic, rolling her eyes, as if to say, *See what I have to put up with?*

"I'm sure it's an astonishing story." Dominic perched on the windowsill.

"It is. My mother used to tell me about him." She smiled. "Only last week she mentioned his name."

That last phrase seemed to knock all Dominic's enthusiasm for six. "And what did she say?" he asked, tentatively.

"That Lawson was the only person who'd survived from the wreck. He was washed ashore in that bay, the one near the house. A local girl took a shine to the lad and insisted her family care for him. He was supposed to be a handsome chap," she added, "almost as nice as you."

Dominic, blushing, appealed with a grimace to Morgan for his rescue.

"What happened to Lawson, Mum? Did this girl whisk him off to the nearest preacher?"

"The little minx would have loved to. And don't you go looking at me as if I'm talking nonsense." She squirmed nervously in her chair. "I had the story from my mother and she'd had it from hers back almost to when Noah was a boy."

"But did this girl succeed? In getting Lawson to marry her?" Morgan hurried the conversation on. If this was a genuine memory, they had to access it quickly.

"No, she didn't. Cantankerous bitch tried to trap him, but she was foiled."

Dominic cast an anxious glance at Morgan, who simply shook his head. When his mother used even the mildest of swear words, then they were on a slippery slope. Still, they had to press on. "So what happened to foil her? Did John Lawson run away?"

"John Lawson?" She turned to Dominic, then Morgan, alternating between the two like a spectator on the centre court at Wimbledon.

"Yes, John Lawson."

She wrinkled her brow. "Is he a friend of yours?"

There seemed no point in continuing down that line. They changed the subject to knitting, but it became increasingly difficult to re-engage Morgan's mother's attention and, after a particularly long and painful period of silence, they said their good-byes.

They didn't discuss the visit once they were back in the car. Morgan made sure Dominic had a map so he could find the back route, in order to avoid some road works which had popped up on the normal road to Porthkennack. That occupation and a stream of small talk kept them occupied all the way to their destination, but for the walk to the seat overlooking Barras Bay, silence took over again.

Eventually Morgan had to say something or burst.

"What a mess, eh? With Mum, I mean." It was a beautiful day and the sun streaming over the pleasure craft in the distance should have raised their spirits, but Morgan's mood was beyond the reach of the magic of sunshine and blue skies. "I'm sorry."

"It's not *your* fault, any of it." Dominic shivered, despite the mild weather. "God preserve us all from a frail old age."

"I wouldn't mind if she *was* old," Morgan said, kicking at stones by his feet for want of anything else to vent his anger on. "She's only in her early sixties. She should be in the prime of her life, like . . . like her." He pointed at a slim, well-dressed woman, walking along the path, who must have been about his mother's age, yet was evidently still full of zest. "It's so bloody unfair."

"Of course it is. Since when was life anything but?"

Silence reigned once more, broken only by the squawking of gulls, until Dominic piped up again. "Do you think she was simply humouring me with that stuff about Lawson surviving? I don't want to be chasing wild gooses."

"Geese." Morgan smiled, despite his gloomy mood. "Trouble is I have no idea. I was there a couple of months back and she started to go on about some money she'd put in a box up in the loft. I thought it was nonsense, until one day when I was bored, and went up there. I found two hundred quid in a box. Exactly as she'd said. Next time I saw her and asked what she wanted me to do with the money, she stared at me like I was talking Urdu."

"So maybe the story about John really is true. And if he survived, then Captain Watson couldn't have conspired to kill him. Not sure how we'll ever prove it, though." Dominic flapped his hand at a seagull which had come a bit too close.

Morgan slapped his knees. "My uncle might know. Well, he's not actually my uncle, just an old friend of Mum's. I don't see him as often as I should these days." Too much awkwardness lurking there, her shade always in the room with them.

Dominic started, like a greyhound hearing the sound of the hare whizzing past the starting traps. "Do you think I should ask him?"

"It's worth a shot." Morgan tried to overcome the guilt he'd feel about turning up, out of the blue, to ask Harry Tressider a string of questions when he'd hardly made contact other than a Christmas card this last year. He told himself it was all for Dominic's sake; he'd see if his conscience fell for it. "Come on. We won't have far to find him, if we're lucky. What does your mate Jack Aubrey say? There's not a moment to lose!"

"I wish he was my mate," Dominic replied, as they headed along the front. "Take that any way you wish."

"Chance would be a fine thing. I bet young Lawson wasn't as much of a looker as Russell Crowe."

"If he was, no wonder that woman fancied him."

The conversation about naval films—the good, the bad, and the downright ridiculous—lasted until they took a sharp left turn away from the sea towards a small side road.

"Does Harry like mountaineering?" Dominic grimaced at the sloping street in front of them.

"You're out of condition. Get a move on."

The terraced house up the back lane was neat, well-kept—and empty.

"I knew it would be too much like good luck." Dominic, clearly unhappy at the uphill hike he'd had to make, kicked at the doorstep. "Things like this never work out for me."

"Oh ye of little faith," Morgan said, pulling back from the door after his fourth attempt on the bell. "He's a creature of habit, so if he isn't here, then he's down at the pub. The Sea Bell. Do you know it?"

Dominic shrugged. "Doesn't ring a bell."

Morgan whacked his arm. "It's not far; enough of a walk to blow the cobwebs away. Downhill all the way, I promise."

The Sea Bell was everything an authentic fisherman's pub should be. A bit dark and dingy with nothing like the promise of live sport to entice in the grockles, but it had a decent reputation among the locals for serving proper beer and proper food. Morgan and Dominic were hardly through the door when a voice boomed through the air.

"Morgan, you tyke. What the bloody hell brings you here?" Harry came bounding over to give him a bear hug, almost cracking his ribs in the process.

"Researching family histories, for a start. Got a pal here, Dominic, who needs to pick a sensible brain. And, for another reason, the need to buy you a pint—I've put it off too long." Hugely relieved at his reception, Morgan dug into his pocket for his wallet.

"That's the sort of thing I like to hear." Harry turned, offering his hand to Dominic. "Pleased to meet you."

"And you." Dominic took the large, gnarled hand, and shook it vigorously. "Any friend of Morgan's . . . as they say."

"Spot on. Now, Morgan, these family stories." Harry winked at Dominic as they went over to the bar to get their order in. "Clean ones or dirty?"

"Ask him. He's the one researching them. I'll get the drinks." Morgan caught the barman's eye and placed his order.

"They're clean, I hope, although if there's scandal to be rooted out, don't spare my innocent ears," Dominic said.

He's off again. Morgan shook his head. "What are you having, Dominic?"

"Sort Mr. Tressider out first."

Morgan grinned. "Oh, I know what he's drinking, unless the leopard's changed its spots. A pint of Chough's Nest. *You're* the unknown quantity."

"I'll have a pint of Chough's Nest too, please. Couldn't come to Porthkennack and not indulge."

The barman opened his mouth, but Harry cut off any comment by raising his hand. "None of your jokes about how he's said it."

Morgan clapped Dominic's shoulder. "They like to tell the grockles they've said it wrong, however they pronounce it."

"Ay, and you've spoken like a native, although I'm guessing you're not from your accent." Harry wrinkled his brow. "Where did you get a taste for the local brew? Don't tell me they sell it up in London."

"No such luck. We used to come here on holiday, years ago. When I was a little boy my greatest ambition was to return as an adult and have a pint of what my father and uncle always drank. Thanks," Dominic added, as Morgan passed him his pint. "I'd been allowed a sip from their glasses when my mum wasn't looking and always had a hankering for more."

"And did it live up to expectations?" Morgan gestured at the barman to pour another pint for Harry, and one for him.

Dominic rolled his eyes. "Isn't the answer obvious, if I'm still ordering it? We didn't drink here, though."

"Very few visitors do." Once the other beers were on the bar, Harry picked up his own glass, then led them to the table he was ensconced at, commanding a view of the street. "This story you want, I assume young Morgan here failed at providing it for you?"

"I'm afraid that's right, although he helped me along the trail."

Morgan suddenly saw a potential problem, looming large, one he should have foreseen before haring off here. Dominic was bound to mention his mother and her story about Lawson. He and Harry had never properly discussed Mum's condition, both of them finding it too painful to tackle beyond a superficial level. He wasn't ready for a heart-to-heart here and now, but it turned out he'd underestimated Dominic. Again.

"It's about the *Troilus*. I'm researching the wreck, and I've run across a rumour that one of the midshipmen who'd sailed on her may have survived." Dominic sailed on himself, with no mention of Morgan's mother or her possible flights of fancy. Harry followed Dominic's account of his interest in the ship, and John Lawson in particular, nodding and chipping in with questions as he went along. Dominic took a swig of beer before finishing up with, "The key bit is proving that he wasn't murdered by the man who was probably his father."

"Right, so what do you want from me?"

"I guess I was hoping you'd say 'Aha, I know all about Lawson' and go on to tell me what really happened." Dominic frowned, like a child who'd opened the biggest box at Christmas only to find that some idiot had filled it with nothing but tissue paper.

Morgan couldn't help leaping in, with a glance at Dominic to try to excuse the economy with the truth he was about to indulge in. "It's *my* fault. I said I thought I'd heard some story, when I was a boy, about there being one survivor of the wreck. Bloke got himself entangled with a local girl or something. Maybe it's my imagination."

"No such thing." Harry took a deep draught of beer, then waited. There'd always been a theatrical touch about the man, over and above his penchant for the girls who did the summer shows down in Newquay.

"He used to do this when we were little," Morgan said, rolling his eyes at Dominic.

"What did I used to do?" Harry jabbed Morgan in the ribs.

"Arse about. Tell us half a story, then leave us waiting for the tagline. Pretend that you didn't know it was our birthdays and then produce a present. Be generally annoying."

"If we're bandying insults, then maybe I'll forget all about that story." Harry, winking at Dominic, was clearly having a whale of a time, irrespective of the months since Morgan had last been in touch.

"You know you won't. Once I've suffered long enough, you'll tell us everything." Morgan gave an exaggerated yawn. "He doesn't keep up the pretence for too long. He thinks the world of us, really."

"Maybe I think the world of *you*. I'll reserve verdict on your brother." Harry took another draught of beer. "Right. John Lawson. Are you sure the story you've got concerns him and not someone else?"

"That's what the ship's muster says." For the first time, when talking about the *Troilus*, Dominic seemed uncertain. "Is there some dispute?"

Harry shrugged. "It's not quite the name I heard about. Rawson, not Lawson. I suppose it could simply be a case of Chinese whispers."

Funny how Harry didn't sound quite so rough and ready, so deep inside his Cornish accent, as he'd done when they'd entered the pub. This must be serious stuff.

"Maybe." Dominic's brow furrowed. "Or there was some deliberate subterfuge at work. Perhaps he changed his name to distract attention from himself."

"Why would he do that?" Morgan asked, but the wheels of communication didn't need oiling. Harry and Dominic had clicked; he sat back and listened, enjoying the show.

"How can we tell at this far a remove?" Harry ran his index finger along the edge of the table. "Trouble is we don't know too much for certain when you get into this research lark. All you've got to go on is dusty old records and stories that have been passed down and embroidered in the retelling. They say that Rawson—Lawson, whoever—was rescued by a girl and her father. She set her cap at him."

Dominic gave Morgan a satisfied glance; so some of his mother's memories were still spot on. "What happened? Did he manage to evade said cap?"

"So the story went. They say he upped and did a moonlit flit, got himself onto a fishing boat or other craft at the harbour and she was left with a broken heart." Harry finished the last of his beer and put the glass down with a thump. "Which is a load of nonsense, of course."

"She dumped *him*, or something?" Morgan asked, finishing his own beer and regretting that having to drive home meant that another pint wasn't going to be a good idea.

"Maybe. Maybe dumped him over a cliff."

"What?" Dominic, who'd started to slump in his chair under the mellowing influence of Chough's Nest, sat bolt upright.

"Or perhaps she just lured him into a nice inaccessible cave— promise of delights to come and all that—and then stabbed him." Harry beamed, as though he were telling some hilarious joke, although it was clear he was in deadly earnest. "She murdered him and told everyone he'd gone off and left her forlorn. No wonder they never found him."

"And it would explain why there's no record of him later in life, which is how the murder conspiracy started in the first place." Dominic sipped his beer, pensively. "Is there any official record of events here? Was she brought to trial?"

"Was she, my arse. She lived into a wicked old age, scaring all the children—they thought she was a witch, and maybe they were right." Harry got up. "Another drink?"

"Half for me, please. And the rest of the story, on the side." Dominic sounded unusually forceful—although maybe that was Chough's Nest's doing.

"Half for me too," Morgan added, feeling like a bit of a spare part when the other two were getting on so well. "Want a hand?"

"I had my hands full of pints when you were barely out of nappies. I'll manage."

"Do you think this story's true, or is he winding me up?" Dominic whispered, when Harry was out of earshot. "And if he isn't, how has he come across this story of her killing Lawson?"

"You'll find out soon enough." Morgan wrinkled his nose. "That story could be true, you know. Handed down from father to son like the tale of our beams was. Or at least it could be the case that Harry believes it to be true, which may not be exactly the same thing."

"If there's a chance there's a speck of authenticity in this story, I have to know about it." Dominic's mouth had a determined set again, that "greyhound in the slips" expression which seemed to come any time something new cropped up. "Even if I can research the story to prove or disprove it once and for all. That ship means a lot to me."

Morgan stared out at the harbour. "She means a lot to me too." He turned, to see Harry returning, hands full. "Thanks for these. We're glad you're back, and not on account of the beer. We've got unanswered questions. Did the lovelorn girl and our young sailor produce any issue, do you know?"

"I don't have the foggiest. Parish records might have something, though."

Dominic nodded. "That's where I'd be inclined to look next. I'd want to find out as much as I can about *her*, too."

"I can help with that. She was called Mary Lusmoore. The family still live round here but I'd steer clear of them." Harry dropped his voice. "Always been troublemakers."

"How the hell do you know that?" Dominic asked.

"Everybody knows they're troublemakers," Morgan confided.

"I'll take your word for *that*, but I was asking how you knew *her* name."

Harry shrugged. "When I was a boy, my granddad used to say that if I didn't behave myself, old Mary Lusmoore would get me and tip me over the cliff."

Morgan and Dominic shared a swift glance; this was either the most useful—and peculiar—lead, or Harry was playing a trick of epic proportions on them.

"Oh, come on." Morgan shook his head. "I've never heard that before."

"You never met my granddad. And anyway, maybe the Capells didn't know the tale." Harry turned to Dominic. "This is a Tressider saying."

Morgan still wasn't convinced. "We'll see if we can find out at the museum. They've got a library of local history."

"You do that." Harry didn't seem perturbed that his word was being questioned. "They'll have all sorts of things you might want to read, youngster."

Dominic nodded. "I've been there once, but that was only to look at the sea stuff. I need to explore the land side."

"Well, don't spend all your time with a nose in dusty old record books. That's no way to live your life. Enjoy it while you can."

"I will." Dominic gave Morgan a fleeting smile. "I promise."

CHAPTER
ELEVEN

Morgan took his guest back to the car park a different way, exploring yet another part of the town that Dominic said he hadn't visited—or, if he had, couldn't remember. At the lane end, a typical Porthkennack transformation occurred, the row of terraced houses giving way to neat, pastel-painted cottages, which retailed at twice the price of the red-bricked equivalent Harry owned.

"Artist's quarter. As opposed to the artists' commune up near me." Morgan rolled his eyes. "Very popular in the days of Henry Scott Tuke."

"Really? His sorts of subjects?"

"No. Ships and seascapes rather than boys and bathing."

"Hm." Dominic eyed up a particularly pretentious property. "Probably the same people who produced that travesty of a painting in Quick's museum. Curse the lot of them."

They walked on, Morgan trying to estimate the property prices. "What chance have you got of running to ground anything about Mary Lusmoore?"

Dominic shrugged. "Lawson, like many a young middie, was easy to keep tabs on up to the time of his last voyage. Ships' musters, diaries, letters, despatches, and the like. Less easy for a local girl of no notable family, although there are always some bits of evidence that will have survived, especially if you have names to work with. Parish registers. Bibles with the family all listed there."

Morgan remembered his grandmother having such a big, black family bible, although he had no idea where it might have gone. "It would be good to turn up a nice piece of evidence that's lain hidden for donkey's years."

"I'm afraid that only happens in books and films. This is real life and not quite so obliging with plot twists."

"Does *nobody* turn up obscure clues in real life?" Morgan appreciated he was out of his depth with anything to do with research.

"I guess if they're in the right place at the right time. Like I was when I got given your phone number," Dominic added, blushing.

"Right time, right place for me too, then." They shared a contented smile. "Will you stay here those extra few days? Looking for Lawson and his lady love?"

"That's a painful amount of alliteration." Dominic slipped his arm across Morgan's shoulders as they strolled along. "I'd certainly like to. Not least to spend time with you, if that's okay. Although I appreciate that you've got a business to run, so I wouldn't be offended if you wanted me to use that hotel room I've got booked."

"Daft bugger." Morgan punched his lover's ribs. "We can work something out. I can always get on with business while you're out chasing sailors. Where will you start your enquiries?"

"Back at the museum. Assuming it's open tomorrow."

"It should be, on a Sunday in what might count as summer. Mind you, I bet the place they store the documents won't. That might have to wait until Tuesday or Wednesday."

"Okay. I should spend an hour or two poking around the internet, now I have this new twist to the tale, but that can wait until you're checking your emails or whatever. Like your uncle said, we should enjoy ourselves."

"I like the cut of your jib! And his. Ice cream. We need ice cream."

"Mr. Whippy. With a flake. From a van."

"It's a deal."

Not far from the car park was a little green, with a paddling pool—still empty given that it was a touch too early in the season—and play equipment which saw action all the year round, even in the depths of winter. The ice cream van sometimes turned up then, dispensing hot drinks, but this bright Saturday it had a short queue of people in search of lollies and choc ices. Morgan and Dominic waited for their turn to purchase a couple of "ninety-nines," then ate them as they strolled, the warm sun on their backs and making them hurry with their eating, as the soft ice cream began to drip onto the cornet.

"What if you never find a definitive answer about Lawson?" Morgan asked between licks. "Is it a problem if we never run the facts to ground?"

If Dominic had noticed the unintentional change from *you* to *we*, he didn't show it. "I may not need to be able to prove she killed him. So long as I can show Captain Watson didn't. And I'm really enjoying the thrill of the chase."

"'The thrill of the chase'?" A quest. Dominic didn't seem like the quixotic type, feet apparently too firmly stuck on the ground for that malarkey, although there was clearly a touch of the romantic in him when it concerned his beloved ship. But what if the quest turned out to be an impossible dream?

"Why not?" Dominic reached over with his ice-cream-less hand and squeezed Morgan's arm. "Searching for Lawson brought me here, didn't it? Facilitated me meeting you. That's reward enough. And if I establish the truth too quickly, it'll eliminate the need to keep returning here."

"Daft bugger. You'll keep coming back. You know that." Morgan transferred his cornet to his other hand so he could return the squeeze. "I'll rephrase the question, then. Is it a problem if you *do* solve the mystery, seeing that the thrill's in that chase?"

"No." Dominic waved his cornet, sending a sprinkling of ice cream in all directions. "Other questions will crop up. There's always another stone to turn."

"And will you keep on turning every stone and never stop?"

"Do you do nothing but ask questions? Trying to cross all the *T*s leads to mad—obsession. I'm not that fanatical."

"Glad to hear it." Glad to hear Dominic swop the word he'd clearly intended using for something that didn't cut quite so close to home too.

"There'll always be another lead to follow, another midshipman's history to dig up or some obscure letter from two hundred years ago to be clarified. Endless possibilities."

"I envy you." That wasn't a word of a lie. To find contentment in such simple things, to always have another corner to go round and so much satisfaction in the journeying. "I don't think I've ever felt an equivalent passion for anything."

"Then you've not run across *it* yet. Maybe you're like your dad. I'm guessing, from what you said, that he never found the one that really kept his interest."

"Perhaps he never would have done. I don't believe it was in his nature to settle for one permanent interest. Apart from family, that is. I wouldn't want you to think he ever tired of us."

Dominic, who'd pushed the last piece of chocolate flake into the middle of the ice cream, demolished it, made short work of the cornet at the point they appeared in sight of the sea again. "You're so lucky. All this on your doorstep every day, rather than a couple of times a year."

Morgan was about to argue that it soon palled, that when he'd been in London he'd regretted—or perhaps felt obliged to regret—how many experiences he must have missed growing up so far from "the action." Now he valued what he had. "I know. I'm learning to count my blessings. Just about."

"Glad to hear it. This is a special place."

This conversation could get mawkish; Morgan concentrated on fishing out his handkerchief to clean his sticky fingers. "Let's get home, grab a bite to eat, and get googling."

Unfortunately, Google kept drawing a blank. The Lusmoore name cropped up plenty of times, but mainly concerning the present generation and usually concerning some manner of shady dealings. Of a Mary Lusmoore who might have been a witch, and her connections with a sailor, there was nothing tangible, although perhaps Morgan and Dominic hadn't worked out the magic combination of words to put into the search engine. Eventually, they put the iPad on standby and settled for a cup of tea and using their own brain cells.

"Why do you murder somebody?" Dominic asked.

If the question was semirhetorical, it was still going to get an answer. "Passion. Or money. At least that's what it usually seems to boil down to in books and on the telly. When it's not getting your mitts on the loot."

"I'm not sure Lawson had any loot. Maybe something came ashore from the wreck along with your timbers, but that would have been fair game for all the beachcombers. She couldn't have put dibs on it."

Morgan smiled; he'd not heard that expression in years. They had always been putting dibs on things at school. "Okay, but Lawson was of good family. He must have been due to come into an inheritance from his father—or fathers, if you think Captain Watson was the natural one and another in the eyes of the law."

"So what was her motive to kill him when she did?" Dominic frowned. "Wouldn't it have been better to keep him alive until he'd inherited? Then tip him over the cliff or whatever?"

"Hm. Good point. What if she thought he would inherit, and then it turned out he was stony broke?"

"Woman thwarted in her ambitions?" Dominic made a throat-slitting gesture, which was less threatening than funny. "You're clutching at straws."

"Okay, so what about jealousy? That's another standard motive. No straw clutching there."

"He had a sailor's roving eye and she didn't like where it was straying?" Dominic cradled his mug while he mulled the notion over. "Maybe. Plenty of strong emotions on your checklist. What about anger?"

"The sudden irrational desire to tip someone over a cliff because they hacked you off? I've known exactly how that feels." Morgan smirked: he'd had the same idea about James once or twice. If there had been a cliff (and the rat himself) handy when the Dear John letter had arrived, James would have been over it like his namesake up a drainpipe. "There are plenty of possible motives, although I don't suppose we're ever going to be able to tell at this distance what actually happened. If everybody knew she'd done it and could prove the fact, wouldn't she have been brought to justice? Especially if Lawson was reasonably well connected. Which also begs the question of whether he tried to contact his family to let them know he'd survived, which he mustn't have done if the rumour started that he'd been killed before he even set sail."

"Perhaps he was too unwell initially to write a letter or have word sent. Maybe, as he recovered, she prevented him. Assuming what we've been told is true, that she wanted him for herself." Dominic twirled his cup around. "It's all theories and gossip and nothing substantial, isn't it?"

"Except for the uniform in the museum," Morgan pointed out. "Anyway, so long as you don't go writing a book about him based on no evidence, then you can indulge in as many theories and as much gossip as you want."

"Okay." Dominic appeared delighted to allow his imagination free rein. "What about spite, as a strong emotion?"

"Go on." Morgan appreciated how frustrating it could be when fate—or other people—seemed determined to hand you a duff deal. "Where's this thread going?"

"Down the line of Mary Lusmoore turning into a strange, spiteful old woman. I can imagine a scenario where Lawson felt under an obligation to her and her family, because they'd saved his life. He wanted to repay her, yet kicked against that responsibility."

"That makes sense, especially if he was a young man who'd been brought up to do his duty. But that sounds like a motive for him to simply up and run away, or to do *her* in, rather than the other way round."

"But what if he couldn't *do her in*? What if he was scared of her because he'd seen a dangerous streak in her personality?" Dominic closed his eyes, as though transporting himself back to those days in search of some clue.

Fear. Yes, Morgan could sympathise with all-consuming terror, something that would make the most reasonable of people act wildly out of character. Like run out of a house in the middle of the night.

"Maybe he wasn't the innocent victim we've assumed he was," Dominic continued, shaking Morgan from thoughts of dreams and visions. "Perhaps he made her life hell, till she could take no more. Or he attacked her and she defended herself."

"Then why not plead self-defence? I can't believe that the past Lusmoores were any less keen than the present ones to get what they were entitled to. Typical of them to cover things up, though. By whatever means."

"By making threats or by oiling palms?"

"Whatever it takes. Or took." Morgan drained his tea. "Sounds like I'm slandering them, but you saw what was on Google about the family."

"Why bother with all that, though?" Dominic ran his hand through his hair. "You could say Lawson had run away to sea again. Or fallen over a cliff and disappeared. Lay on the grief with a trowel and maybe you get away with it."

"Enough speculation. My head hurts." This wasn't going to end up with a definite conclusion. As frustrating as reading a murder mystery with the crucial last few pages missing. "No Lawson talk until you've done some further research. There's sport on the telly and a pair of sea bass in the fridge for tea. If you don't fancy that, then you can lock yourself away with your laptop while I have forty winks on the sofa."

"I'll join you."

Dominic didn't just join Morgan for a kip on the settee or to help cook dinner; it had been unspoken but inevitable that he'd be sharing the man's bed too. Sex wasn't the be all and end all of life, although the initial madness of passion still burned bright, even if Morgan felt guilty about dragging Dominic into his mess of a life. But they were both grown-up, both knew their own minds, both had presumably entered into things with their eyes open.

They'd gone upstairs in a statelier fashion than they'd done the night before, Dominic snuggling down with one of his naval books—naturally—while Morgan performed his ablutions. He'd picked up a thriller, and they'd read together by the light of the bedside lamp until Morgan could hardly keep his eyes open.

Morgan jolted awake as Dominic rescued the thriller from where it had dropped from Morgan's hands onto his chest.

"Didn't mean to wake you."

"Didn't mean to doze off."

"No worries. You look washed out."

"That's your fault. Rogering me stupid." Morgan nestled closer. The night had turned surprisingly nippy, where the wind had veered, making his exposed arm feel like ice. "You carry on and don't mind me."

"I'm ready to turn in, myself." Dominic carefully marked his place in his book, then placed it on the bedside table, turning off the light before settling down with his arm over Morgan's shoulder. "Been a long day."

"Been a good day." Morgan relaxed into the embrace. "Could be another good night, if you want."

"Is that an offer I'd ever refuse? Not that I'm sex mad." Dominic chuckled. "I've had my leg over more this last month than the previous six."

"Much the same here." Morgan brushed his lips along his lover's skin. "Good thing you found my address, wasn't it?"

"You can say that again." A great sigh passed through Dominic's chest. "It's a shame you don't live around the corner. Or at the other end of the District line."

"I wouldn't wish for that. I remember what the Tube is like. It can take as long to get from one side of London to the other as to fly to Spain."

Dominic, shifting awkwardly in the bed, murmured, "I wasn't dropping an unsubtle hint. I know you can't move. Not with your mum as she is."

Not with work or friendships or a hundred other things, either. But distance did add another complication to the pot.

"I know it's early days too, so don't think I'm rushing you again," Dominic continued, evidently unaware of displaying an uncanny ability to read Morgan's mind. Although Morgan found this faculty vaguely comforting; it was much easier to be known than to be misunderstood. "I was simply stating a fact about the distances involved."

"Point taken." This conversation needed diverting elsewhere, and the most effective way to do that was appealing to Dominic's romantic side. So Morgan manoeuvred into a suitably comfortable position, sharing a kiss that was sweet enough to be taken as a "good night" yet passionate enough to be acted on if the mood took them.

Which it did. It seemed natural now to give in to their mutual attraction and shared passion, to shove any worries to the back of his brain. Why not live for the moment?

CHAPTER TWELVE

Sunday morning was set aside for a lie in, brunch, and a visit to the museum, in that order. Morgan "passed" on the last of the three, ostensibly as he had groceries to get in but mainly because the conversation of the night before refused to stop nagging at him. It wouldn't be healthy to live in each other's pockets, irrespective of that early-relationship desire to be with the other every minute. To give in to that temptation, the slogging east and west across the country every weekend, would wear them out. And Morgan's recent experience of a long-distance relationship wasn't encouraging.

By the time he got to one o'clock, though, he was itching to get in the car and drive to their rendezvous—a small car park on the coast south of Porthkennack next to a great café, much frequented by locals and hopefully not yet overrun by grockles.

He'd not long been in the car park when Dominic's Yaris appeared, pulling up in the place next to his Audi. By the eager grin plastered over his gob, Dominic had to have something important to share.

"Any luck?" Morgan asked, as they got out of their cars.

"Possibly, or possibly not." Dominic smirked.

"How useless a researcher are you? That's no academic sort of an answer."

"I think it's a highly academic sort of an answer." Dominic tapped on his car bonnet like a lecturer emphasising some point. "Life is rarely cut-and-dried."

"Oh, it's going to be like that, is it? You'd better explain it in words of one syllable. Over lunch, preferably." The café was convenient, comfortable, and gave a stunning view over the sea. No part of the District line could offer anything as good. It was warm enough for taking drinks and sandwiches outside too. A couple of bottles of cold beer on the table and they could get back down to business.

"This is all right, isn't it?" Dominic took a draught, then admired the beer he'd poured into his glass. "This'll lubricate the brain. Anyway, the lady at the museum had never heard of a local saying about Mary Lusmoore, and none of the books in the gift shop seemed to mention her. And flicking through them was a major act of subterfuge, under the beady eye of the man at the till."

"I bet. I think he's been there since Noah came out of the ark. Bite your leg if you dare to leave a corner dog-eared."

"Tell me about it. I had to visit there three times, and buy something each go. My niece and nephew will be delighted. Exactly the kind of tat I'd have enjoyed at their age. Anyway, I asked the lady about local records, and she said I couldn't get access before Tuesday, so I've made an appointment." Dominic knocked back his beer, appreciatively.

"I'm guessing that, as regards luck, that was the 'possibly not' bit." Morgan savoured his own drink; bottled Italian beer, not as meaty as a pint of Chough's Nest, but wonderfully refreshing on a warm afternoon. "What's the 'possibly'?"

"Our grumpy friend in the gift shop was grilling me about what I was up to, so I had to tell him. He reckons there's an old poem about the wreck, or Mary Lusmoore, or both, in the archives."

"Hm. Are you sure that story isn't an embellishment one of your 'helpful' volunteers came up with to secure a repeat visit?"

"Spoilsport. I'll find out on Tuesday. I'm also hoping there might be something in the archives about the provenance of that uniform."

"Don't hold your breath about the reliability of the archives on anything. Dad always used to say that you have to take all the local history with a pinch of salt. Or maybe a dirty great sack full. Unless you trust the sources."

"Your dad was very wise." Dominic swirled the remains of his beer around the glass. "So where's going to be reliable?"

"We could try one of the local churches. We're unlikely to be able to poke through the registers today—anyway most of the old stuff is probably at the county archive—but the graves go back a long way. They're not all legible."

Dominic's eyes shone. "I've got my rubbing equipment in the car. Sometimes that brings the writing up."

"Great. Now we only need to know where the Lusmoores bury their kin."

"The Lusmoores?" The café owner—who'd come out to clear away used crockery off the tables—piped up. "Sorry. Wasn't listening in."

"Never thought you were." Morgan grinned.

"If you want Lusmoore plots, they're all up at the new cemetery."

Morgan shivered; that was where his dad had been laid to rest. He said, hastily, "That's too recent for us. You wouldn't happen to know where we can find any older ones? Victorian or further back."

The café owner blew out her cheeks. "I think there might be some at that old church, on the Harlyn road. The one they tarted up and reopened a few years back. Not far from the recycling centre."

Dominic thanked the woman for her help, then glanced at Morgan. "Do you know where that is?"

"I can get us to the recycling centre. You can navigate once we're there."

"Sounds like the blind leading the blind," the cafe owner said witheringly over her shoulder as she took the cutlery she'd collected back inside, so she didn't hear Dominic's response of "She knows us too well," or see him almost wetting himself with laughter.

Morgan shared the laughter, and an affectionate glance. How could he have ever contemplated not inviting this guy back, and where would he have been if he hadn't?

The churchyard—which was easy to find, blind or not—appeared surprisingly overgrown, although a statement on the notice board by the lychgate informed them this wasn't neglect but part of a scheme to encourage wild flowers to grow. Nobody seemed to be around, apart from a woman tending one of the plots, and another notice stated that the church itself was only used on the first Sunday morning of the month, while the bulk of services took place at the newer church which had sprung up to serve the burgeoning Porthkennack population and which didn't suffer from dry rot and—literally—bats in the belfry. There was a sheet of paper telling people all about *them* too; somebody in the church must have either had too much time on their hands or an unhealthy penchant for informational posters.

Morgan and Dominic decided to separate, working logically from opposite corners, scouring up and down through the plots, letting each other know if they found any Lusmoores, so that Dominic could take a wealth of photos to pore over at home. At least that was the plan, but the family proved hard to track down—as elusive in death as in life—until Morgan stumbled across a single plot, surprisingly well tended given that it dated from late in Queen Victoria's reign. He waved Dominic across, not wanting to shout in this particular location.

"Hopefully this is the first of several." Dominic got out his camera to take a picture of the headstone, which was just about legible: Harold and his wife, who might have been Ellen. "There's no logic to what's where in this place."

"No. I can't see any more Lusmoores around this grave. I guess there are worse ways to spend a Sunday afternoon, though." The sun was on their backs, the birds singing in the trees, not a grockle in sight.

"Glad you're not bored off your face." Dominic put his camera away and wandered back to his own search sector, without waiting for a response. Morgan had to admit that he *wasn't* bored. The search for Lawson was intriguing, especially when it steered clear of ships. A recollection of his nightmare sent a chill through his bones, but he shook it off.

As it turned out, maybe he should have heeded that as a warning, but he got back to the hunt, going along the line of gravestones, stooping here and there to read the weathered inscriptions. He'd felt fine all day, other than a slight ringing and discomfort in his ears as he kept bending and straightening again, so the devastating rush of symptoms, when it came, felt like an express train hitting. The sudden wave of dizziness and nausea, the sensation that some idiot had taken the churchyard and made it spin like a merry-go-round, the panic at not knowing what the bloody hell was going on, almost floored him. He managed to stagger to a convenient tomb, then parked his backside on it, waiting for the world to stop whizzing round.

Dominic rushed over, but his voice, distant and unclear, sounded like it was echoing from inside a well. At last Morgan made out that he was being asked what was wrong.

"How the hell do I know?" he managed to whisper, trying to force his eyes to focus.

Dominic knelt in front of him, putting his hand on Morgan's knee. "What are your symptoms? Apart from looking like death?"

"Dizzy. Can't see or hear properly." Morgan ran a hand across his brow, finding it clammy and cold. "Feel like I might puke. You're right in range."

Dominic's grip on Morgan's knee tightened, but he neither flinched nor moved. "Should I ring for an ambulance?"

"No, I'll be all right in a minute." Morgan wasn't certain he believed that, but he didn't want to get the emergency services over if he wasn't in danger. Although how did he know if he was in danger or not? He didn't have pain in his arm or chest, so this couldn't be a heart attack, could it? Stroke? He flexed his hands, but they both responded equally.

"You don't give the impression of being all right. Are you sure I shouldn't run you to casualty?"

"I'm sure. Don't make a fuss." He didn't seem to be at imminent risk of death. "I had a funny five minutes, that's all."

"Hm." Dominic narrowed his eyes. "Looked like more than that to me."

Morgan shook Dominic's hand away, then tried to get up, but had to sit straight down; if he wasn't on his feet, the world wasn't whirling around him. "Give me a minute or two," he gasped.

"When you're up to it, I'll drive us both home. The graves can wait. We can come back for them—and for your car—when you're feeling better." Dominic patted Morgan's knee again. "Give me your keys and I'll make sure it's all secured."

Morgan was about to protest but then gave in, meekly handing over his key ring. There was no way he should be behind a wheel in this state. And thank God he had Dominic at hand. Had Mum felt like this, when she'd had her fall?

He was slightly less green about the gills by the time they got back home, Dominic having driven calmly and steadily to reduce the vehicle's throwing itself about in the winding lanes. Almost well enough to persuade himself not to ring the doctor, although Dominic wouldn't be swayed. He stood over Morgan while he made the call to the NHS Direct service, the impatient patient praying they wouldn't immediately order him down to the hospital for a once-over. Was he just being stubborn, or did the spectre of his mother's experience still haunt him? Her fall and hospitalisation had been the first steps on a slippery slope.

As they waited for the nurse to ring back, Dominic got Morgan a drink of water and tried to keep them cheerful. "I bet they're not used to locals needing attention on a bank holiday Sunday. Usually grockles with sunburn. Or frostbite." The words might have been humorous, but his pained expression gave him away.

"It'll make a change." Morgan took a sip. The nausea had eased, and his head was clearing, to the point he felt like a bit of a fraud. But the call from the nurse put an end to that. After going through a seemingly endless checklist of symptoms, she said she thought he might have labyrinthitis, although she'd get a doctor to do a phone consultation. At least it wasn't a trip to casualty, but Morgan still didn't relish the experience.

They'd already moved into the lounge, where Morgan could sprawl on the sofa with the landline handset close by. Dominic had pointed out—quite logically—that keeping the mobile free for nonmedical calls would be sensible. If he actually meant that strategy kept an incoming line open for the nursing home if need be, he was too diplomatic to mention it. Morgan shut his eyes and tried to grab a nap, but sleep was too elusive, every little noise making him start, thinking the phone was about to go. After twenty minutes he gave up.

"I've been finding out about this on the internet while you've been having a rest." Dominic scrolled down his laptop's screen. "It's a lot easier to find stuff about labyrinthitis than about John Lawson. I think you may be having it quite easy, compared to some people. You don't have pus coming out of your ears, for a start."

Morgan grimaced. "That really doesn't help my nausea, thank you."

"Sorry. And don't tell me off for using that word. Circumstances alter cases." Dominic came over to perch on the side of the sofa. "You're not a very good patient, are you?"

"Leave off." Morgan frowned. "Can I have a cup of tea?"

"Not until you've spoken to the doctor."

"I'm not likely to need a general anaesthetic, am I?" He tried to look appealing.

"Oh, all right. But stay there. I can find everything." Dominic headed for the kitchen while Morgan carefully readjusted his position. He tried flicking on the television, but the first thing he encountered—a cinema-style advert with flashy, jump-cut photography and blaring music—made him so disoriented he shut the box straight down again. He wasn't sure he could manage something as sedate as watching a cricket match at this rate.

Dominic returned with a steaming mug of tea, which Morgan sipped gratefully while he explained his lack of success with the goggle-box.

"That's no surprise. Most adverts are hard enough to put up with even if you're feeling a hundred percent. If I was prime minister I'd—"

A shrill ringtone interrupted Dominic's sermon.

"That's the doctor, I hope." Morgan grabbed the phone.

After the initial checks, his name and date of birth and all the rest of it gone over yet again, he went through the events in the graveyard, reciting for the third time the list of symptoms, saying yes or no while the doctor explored a list of other questions as he tried to pin down a diagnosis. Had he been ill, with a cold or something similar? Was he under stress or over tired? In the end, the diagnosis of labyrinthitis seemed to be confirmed, and Morgan was advised to have plenty to drink; get plenty of rest; avoid alcohol, bright lights, and loud noise; and generally take care of himself. With the proviso that if his symptoms changed and any alarming signs showed up, he'd go straight to casualty or call an ambulance. Morgan agreed and put the phone down.

"So what's the prognosis?" Dominic asked.

"Keep it till it gets better." Morgan fleshed that out with some of the things the doctor had said. "If need be, he'll give me a course of Valium, but I'd rather not go down that at this point."

"I don't blame you. And I'm appointing myself your nurse. You can lie on that settee the rest of the day, and I'll fetch and carry."

"Am I allowed to get up for a wee or will you provide a bedpan?"

"Goon." Dominic put down his mug. "Your tea will have gone cold. Let me get you a fresh one."

"And biscuits," Morgan pleaded. "No reason I can't have something to keep me going."

"Plain ones, then. You still look like you might puke at any moment."

"Yes, nurse." Morgan shut his eyes, listening to his guest clanking about in the kitchen. The conversation with the doctor had eased his concerns on the threat-to-life front, but his longer-term anxiety remained.

"Did that doctor suggest you went to your own GP to get checked over?" Dominic asked, as he came back into the lounge bearing a tray of goodies.

"No. He reckons if I take it easy for a few days, I should be back to normal. No—" Morgan held up his hand and pointed with his shortcake biscuit "—no comments about me not ever turning out normal."

"Wouldn't dream of it." Dominic chuckled. "Would it be better if I booked into that hotel? Or would you prefer to have me on hand to do the nursing duties?"

"For once I'm going to swallow my pride and say I'd love it if you'd stay. And not just to wait on me hand and foot. I'd like somebody around."

"I get that. I'll ring the hotel tomorrow and tell them. CBA to do it tonight, to be honest." Dominic dunked his biscuit in his tea, then ate it with evident enjoyment. After both giving themselves to nothing other than the sensual pleasures of sipping tea and clearing the biscuit plate, Dominic remarked, with an airiness that wouldn't have fooled anybody, "You didn't mention the nightmare?"

Morgan, suddenly wary, drained his mug before answering. "Why should I? It's not related."

"No-o," Dominic replied, unconvincingly. "I only wondered if the nightmares had made you tired. Might have contributed to the labyrinthitis."

"They might. Except that I haven't had those dreams in weeks."

"Good point." Dominic avoided Morgan's gaze.

"Is that why you were so keen on me seeing a doctor? Because you think I need help? That this funny turn is all linked up to me going loony?"

"I never said that. I never said anything like it." Dominic winced. "I only meant it would be worth getting a proper check over. You've been through the mill and you could be overstressed and run down, at the very least."

"Thanks for the medical advice, Dr. Watson."

"Oh, stop being such an arsehole. I don't need a medical degree to see that you're worrying yourself sick about everything. Be honest with me. Why won't you get some help?"

Morgan opened his mouth, shut it again, then sat in silence, letting his anger subside. "Because I'm scared, can't you see that? Scared of what a proper doctor might tell me."

"Isn't knowing the truth better than torturing yourself with pessimistic self-diagnosis?" Dominic came over, settling himself next to Morgan on the settee to stroke his leg. "My God, you're shaking."

"I know. It isn't funny being me, living in my head." Morgan pressed his hands together between his thighs.

Dominic took them in his own, stilling the trembling. "The chances are this is nothing sinister, neither the dreams or the dizziness, and all the worry has been unnecessary."

Morgan took a deep breath. "All right. I'll make an appointment for next week."

Dominic narrowed his eyes. "Will you really?"

"Don't you trust me?"

"Do I have to answer that? It might incriminate me." Dominic might have been joking, but he was as pale and drawn as if he'd been the one to have been taken ill. "I have half a mind to bundle you in the bloody car on Tuesday and force you to see the GP. But I won't; it's a decision you must make for yourself. Nobody and nothing else can work it."

"Heal myself and all that new-age mumbo jumbo?"

"You're being a dick again." Dominic's sudden smile belied his words. "All I'm saying is that if I made you see the doctor, you'd be going in half cock—shut up sniggering—and would probably clam up when he asked you something too close to home."

"You know me far too well." Morgan sighed. "Okay, I *will* make that appointment, but not until this labyrinthitis has calmed down. I need to get my head clear."

"Hm. Okay."

The determined set of Dominic's face showed Morgan this was a promise he wouldn't be able to wriggle out of, no matter how much he wanted to.

CHAPTER
THIRTEEN

Morgan felt a bit better the next morning—well enough to put away a decent breakfast which Dominic had insisted he eat in bed. He didn't feel dizzy apart from when he stood at the top of the stairs and looked down, but a moment with his eyes shut helped the symptoms pass. Dominic was great, providing precisely the right amount of help and fuss, and arranging to pick up any groceries they needed on the way back from the churchyard, where he was going to finish off his research. He'd arranged for a taxi to take him there and would bring Morgan's car back with him, assuming it still had all its wheels intact.

Morgan was grateful for some time alone to gather his thoughts, telling himself that he'd overreacted the day before. He rang the nursing home to explain that he wouldn't be in for a few days, and got a large dose of sympathy from the duty nurse. She reiterated the advice to avoid driving, to get plenty of rest, not to use any dangerous machinery, "and no climbing ladders or disco dancing," she added cheekily.

"My disco days are long past. Anyway, don't they call it clubbing now?"

"Don't go clubbing either, then. We'll see you when you're better. Don't go hurrying your recovery. We don't want two of you to take care of."

The remark had obviously been meant as a cheery joke, but it didn't do anything for his still-fragile confidence. "Very wise. I'd be far too much trouble."

Morgan ended the call, then went to open his much-neglected inbox. He managed about a half an hour before admitting defeat:

he'd have to wean himself back onto working with screens. He made a cold drink and took it out into the garden, to sit in the sunshine and wait for Dominic's return. The bloke seemed to be taking longer than anticipated; hopefully that was because he'd been successful at the graveyard rather than having found the car with all the tyres nicked.

He must have dozed off, waking with a start and a cricked neck at the sound of a car pulling up onto the drive. "I'm round the back," he shouted when he heard the car door slam, not wanting to get up too quickly in case he fell straight back down again. "Come and join me."

Dominic came around the side of the house. "What if I'd been a burglar?"

"At this time of day? They'll all be tucked up in bed after last night's jobs."

"Car's in one piece, if you were thinking some scrote might have wrecked it." Dominic handed over the keys. "Fancy a cuppa? I'm gagging for one."

"Please. Need any help?"

"No, it's fine. Although if you'd like to supervise me putting away the groceries, that might be a good idea."

"Yeah, okay. Not that I'm obsessed with what goes in which cupboard." Not that he'd admit, anyway. "Actually, let me put the stuff away. I'm not a total invalid."

"Cool beans." Dominic took the bag of groceries inside the kitchen, however.

"Successful day?" Morgan asked, as he stowed away the milk.

"Yep, all round." Dominic beamed as he filled the kettle. "Didn't drive your car into a ditch, got all the shopping, made a bit of progress Lusmoore wise, but that can wait until I've got a mug of tea in my hand."

Morgan's enduring memory of Dominic, once the guy went back to London, was going to be him drinking tea: an image as powerful and endearing as him lying tousled in bed. "Thanks for being so helpful." He kissed Dominic's cheek and went back to the groceries.

"Got to help a mate in need." Dominic, blushing furiously, carried on with making them a drink and something to eat.

They took everything through to the dining room—under those infamous, fateful beams—so Dominic could share the fruits of his morning's labour.

"I couldn't find a grave for Mary Lusmoore. Because it's not there." His eyes danced. "There was this old bloke pottering around who gave the impression he was ancient enough to remember the woman herself. He came over for a chat just as I'd run across a clump of Lusmoore plots."

"You're no doubt irresistible to older men." Morgan chuckled.

"Ha bloody ha. He asked me if I was interested in local history, then took me into the vestry to show me the records. Turns out he was the verger, so had the keys."

"See? He had designs on your body. Didn't your mother ever tell you not to go with strange men?"

"Oh, give it a rest. That funny turn hasn't improved your jokes. He was probably grateful for somebody to talk to."

"Okay." Morgan held his hands up. "What did you learn?"

"That Mary Lusmoore hasn't got a grave because she threw herself over a cliff, up on the headland not far from where *Troilus* went down. Her body was never recovered. She was old by then, and maybe a bit . . ." Dominic blew out his cheeks, clearly searching for words that wouldn't re-ignite the flames of Morgan's distress.

"She'd gone a touch senile? Batty? You can say it, you know. I think we've gone past walking on eggshells."

"Thank God for that." Dominic smiled. "Yeah, let's settle for saying she was 'eccentric.'"

"Eccentric it is. What else did Old Father Time say?"

"That somebody had written a history of the church and its graveyard. I couldn't get a copy because there was only the original there and that must have dated back a hundred years. So close enough to the time of the events to have a reasonable chance of being reliable."

"Shame you couldn't have brought it home." Morgan could imagine how Dominic would have been. A dog with two tails couldn't have matched his delight at finding a new piece of evidence.

"I got a photocopy. They had a little desktop-printer thing that somebody had donated that they used to run stuff off. I got the whole history of the church being modernised, along with some more relevant stuff." He opened the document wallet he kept all his odds and ends in, pulling out a sheet of paper. "Have a shufti."

The page wasn't easy to read, a not-very-good copy of what must have been a fairly illegible original, but Morgan could make out enough to tell it primarily concerned Mary's father, Harold, whose grave he had found. He shrugged off a frisson at the memory of what had followed that discovery, concentrating on Harold's tragic story. Three of his children had pre-deceased him; and Mary—his eldest—had cared for him to the end of his life. That seemed to contradict the story of her being a spiteful woman, unless she'd changed later.

She had fallen to her death some ten years after he died, her cousins saying that it had been a terrible accident but the speculation being that she'd committed suicide, perhaps at never having come to terms with her father's death.

"Sad, isn't it?" Morgan held the text up to a better light. "Do you think she actually threw herself off the cliff in guilt at having killed Lawson?"

"It's as reasonable a theory as any. Or maybe he'd broken her heart and she'd never got over it." Dominic ran his fingers through his hair, making it stand up in untidy spikes. Morgan resisted the temptation to smooth it again; that could wait for an hour or two. "Or perhaps the stories we were told all arose afterwards. Folk trying to explain away why a devoted daughter had turned so odd."

"People love to be wise after the event. Like when somebody commits a murder out of the blue. Everybody says they always had their suspicions."

Dominic nodded. "It would have been worse if they'd had the tabloids back in those times. Or social media."

"Bane of modern life." Morgan handed back the paper. "I wish I'd been able to come with you to get that."

"So do I. I missed having you there to share our triumph, albeit it was a small one."

Morgan noted the *our*, but his recent antagonism at such presumptions was starting to fade. If his funny turn in the churchyard had taught him anything, it was to value what you had to hand when you had it, and let the future sort itself. "Maybe I could come to the museum with you tomorrow? If I promise not to faint?"

Dominic narrowed his eyes. "We'll see how you feel. You're still supposed to be resting."

"I'd like to do something, rather than sit here on my arse. I need to. I want to feel normal again."

"You will feel normal. As normal as you're ever likely to get. Just don't rush things for the sake of a day or two." The endearing expression of concern in Dominic's face went straight from Morgan's eyes to his trousers.

"There's something else I could do, to feel like myself." Morgan left his seat, edged round the table to where Dominic was sitting; he had already turned in his chair, clearly anticipating what was to come. "It takes two."

"Of course it does." Dominic slipped his arms around Morgan's waist to pull him close. "And while my conscience tells me I should be saying no, that it's barely twenty-four hours since you were taken ill, I'm willing to ignore its voice for once."

"That's what I like to hear." Morgan leaned in for a kiss. "I'm feeling fine now, but if you want to help me up the stairs, like I'm an old man, I won't mind."

"Very tempting."

They managed the stairs one by one, Morgan so preoccupied with being kissed he almost forgot to worry whether he'd feel dizzy. When they got to the bedroom and the big, firm bed, their big, firm, and desperate body parts made it plain the time was right to couple again.

It wasn't the most energetic bout of lovemaking he'd ever had, Dominic treating him as though he were made of glass and Morgan trying not to get annoyed at the fact. Once he'd reconciled himself to it, the experience became curiously stimulating, like stepping into a new territory without the aid of maps, or treading through a minefield, each step both dangerous and thrilling. Maybe he'd have to have another funny turn if this was one of the outcomes.

Dominic had suggested a safeword—bloody *Milton Keynes* again—if things became uncomfortable, but it hadn't been needed. They fell into that same routine they'd established: a mixture of doing what they knew the other liked and exploring new options.

Perhaps at least part of the funny turn had been psychological, because once Morgan was lost in lovemaking, he didn't feel the slightest hint of dizziness or anything other than pleasure. Extreme pleasure.

They dozed afterwards, until Morgan came to with a start as a dream of walking with Dominic along the cliffs turned nasty.

"Eh?" Dominic murmured. "Are you having a nightmare?"

"No. Yes. Not the ship dream, anyway." Morgan tried to get the vision clear in his mind, but it was already hazy. "We were up on the cliff path, you and me. You tried to knock me over the edge."

"You're thinking of Mary Lusmoore. Your imagination turns everything into a dream."

"Doesn't everyone's? No, don't answer that, my head's too befuddled." He didn't particularly want to discuss his dreams, his imagination, or whether his brain worked differently to other people's. "I haven't dreamed about *Troilus* since you were here before, and I don't want to risk my thoughts going down that line."

"Okay. I'm banning talk about anything to do with my research today. You can spend the whole evening slagging off James if you want."

"Don't tempt me. I'm not sure it would help my medical condition." Morgan sighed, stretched, and snuggled down again. "Another kip, then you can tell me about your childhood holidays. We talk far too much about me."

And so much introspection didn't help his mental state one bit.

Monday evening had been quiet: a movie on the telly, a meal out of the freezer, and a bed shared companionably, as a result of which Morgan felt better on Tuesday, not having suffered any dizziness since the previous morning. He agreed—reluctantly—to another day indoors, so he didn't jeopardise his recovery. And when Dominic set off in his hire car for his appointment at the museum archives, Morgan had another, more successful, stab at his emails. He managed a bit of work, although the movement of items across the screen became disorienting, forcing him to abandon design in favour of some urgent paperwork. He tried not to entertain the thought that he'd be affected long-term and not be able to return to his business. Why the hell did he have to always look on the bleak side?

As his thoughts were determined to taunt him, he had to show defiance—he could manage to get along just as normal. He decided to make some soup for lunch, to prove that simple things like chopping onions or peeling carrots weren't beyond him, and that he could be trusted with a pan on a hob.

When Dominic returned, he came straight to the kitchen. "Smells good," he said. "Almost as good as you." He landed a butterfly kiss on Morgan's neck.

"Thanks. I hope it tastes okay."

"I'm sure it'll taste as good as you do too."

"Smoothy. Being a nursemaid clearly suits you. You're coming out of your shell." Morgan returned the kiss. "Any luck at the archives?"

"A bit. Mostly they verified what we'd already come across. Which is good in itself, because I never trust any one source. A bit like the internet—you might get lots of mentions of something, but if they all eventually come back to a single source and that's unreliable, you're stuffed."

"That happens with written records too. One naff bit of scientific research gets perpetuated until proven wrong."

Dominic grinned. "Yeah, scientific 'proof' isn't what it's cracked up to be. Like these." He took two eggs from out of the storage rack, then turned them in his hands. "Good for you, bad for you: no idea what the current medical opinion is."

"My opinion is they're about to fall on the floor if you keep jiggling them. I've enough to do without clearing up egg yolk."

"Talking of enough to do, did you make an appointment at the doctor's?" The overly casual question exposed the fact that Dominic must have been dying to ask it.

"Yes. Next Tuesday, because I couldn't pretend it's urgent. Gives me time to screw my courage to the sticking place."

"Yeah, well make sure you don't screw yourself out of it. I'll be ringing that evening for an update."

"Yes, matron."

"I'll bloody 'yes, matron' you if you don't stop it."

"Promises, promises." Morgan slipped his arms around Dominic's waist. "Maybe I need a bed bath or something. Fancy playing nurse?"

"Yes, but not at the moment. I want my lunch. I'll play nurse later if you play kitchen maid now."

"It's a deal." Sex, food, and a joint interest in a small patch of history. There were worse things to base a relationship on.

Morgan happily got on with the last bits of the soup-making, cutting bread, getting out some cheese and the like. He went to wash the cheese board as it had a distinctly dodgy appearance, and caught a glimpse of the distant sea and a hint of a cloud over the Devil's Anvil. It was only once he was back stirring the soup that he realised he hadn't felt uncomfortable seeing that view, hadn't automatically thought of ships and wrecks. Maybe at last, under Dominic's empathetic care, he was getting somewhere in this battle against his thoughts. Maybe he'd make so much progress in the following week that he wouldn't have to confess all at the doctor's, although that could risk Dominic's wrath if his almost telepathic abilities sussed out that Morgan had bottled things again.

"You're rather pensive." Dominic's voice over his shoulder snapped Morgan out of his reverie.

"I'm always pensive. You should know that by now."

"Not when we're in bed." Dominic gently stroked his arm. "You seem really relaxed then."

"That's different." On all counts. "Come on. Lunch."

After they'd eaten, Morgan, feeling constrained at being stuck indoors, insisted they go out into the garden. If Dominic twigged that—against all precedent—Morgan had made them take their chairs to a spot where the rocks were in view, he didn't mention the fact. They sat in the sunshine, poring through what had turned up in the archives.

"Earlier you said what you'd found was 'mostly' verification, but you keep smiling like a cat that's got the cream," Morgan pointed out, with a grin. "So what else did you find?"

"A poem. It's in here somewhere." Dominic rummaged among a pile of documents.

"A poem?"

"Ballad, rather than poem, and not a very good one, either." Dominic brandished a sheet of paper. "More McGonagall than Masefield."

"I see what you mean." Morgan, smoothing out the copy, winced at some of the wording. "Crappier than the stuff you get down the folk club. And that's saying something."

"Are your local groups as bad as that?"

"Aren't they always bad?" Morgan rolled his eyes. "Only fit for students and tourists. Strip away the flowery wording from this, though, and it tells an interesting tale."

"That's what I thought." Dominic nodded. "If this is based on the true story or at least part of that story, it could give us a real clue to what went on."

"Yep." According to the ballad, Mary Lusmoore and Midshipman Lawson tried to get something from the wreck, some treasure she really wanted that had belonged to his mother. He said he'd retrieve it, as a sign of true love. He failed, even when he'd tried the obligatory three times. "It's always three attempts, isn't it? The magic number."

"It wasn't magic for him. He failed, and she went mad." Dominic wrinkled his nose. "That last part might be true. The three attempts I'll take with a pinch of salt. If *Troilus* broke on those rocks, there wouldn't have been much of a hull left to dive onto."

"Exactly. Although the bit about bunging him over the cliff in the very place she later took her own life, full of remorse, might have a grain of truth in it too." Morgan rescanned the ballad, rolling his eyes again at the terrible lyrics. "Are we reading too much into this? Is it any more trustworthy, in terms of real life, than Thomas the Rhymer or whatever?"

"That's what I wondered, all the way home. I was hoping you'd be a voice of reason."

Morgan grinned. "Fat chance of that. Although I've got a reasonable question for you. Does this doggerel predate that book you saw, or postdate it? Are the two from the same source, based on each other or independent?"

"That's about seventeen questions." Dominic took the paper back, peering at it again. "And there's another option: are they both part of somebody trying to drum up a romantic legend that might motivate people to visit the area? Stoking up the tourist trade isn't a new phenomenon. Medieval monks were at it."

"Pretty naff attempt, then, because it didn't work. Porthkennack is hardly overrun with 'Ye Olde Mary Lusmoore tea rooms' or whatever."

"True." Dominic glanced heavenward. "Here, I don't like the look of that."

"I agree." A leaden-grey bank of cloud was blowing in from the Atlantic, threatening to dump its contents sometime in the not-too-distant future. They gathered up their bits and pieces, just making it into the house as the first drops of rain hit the flagstones.

"That's a bloody shame. It was nice getting some fresh air." Morgan grimaced out of the window. "Honest to God, I need to get out for a while, and farther than the garden. I'm getting sick of these four walls."

"Don't try too much, too soon. It's only been a few days you've had to put up with it. You'd have been no use in Colditz, would you?" Dominic's forced chuckle couldn't entirely conceal his concern.

"Maybe I should dig a bloody tunnel under the hedge. I've got to stretch my legs." Morgan grabbed Dominic's arm. "You can drive. I'll let you mother hen me as much as you want. Let's go and do *something*, even if it's having another ice cream in the park."

"Too wet for that, now. What about a pint at the pub? Is that sufficiently leg stretching if we don't park too close to it?"

"That sounds like a great idea. So long as you won't argue if I really do have a pint and not a Diet Coke."

"That's a point. The doctor said no alcohol, right?"

"Spoilsport. Not a chance of a half of mild?"

"Hm. I suppose that should be okay. As long as you lay off the Chough's Nest, and if you feel vaguely woozy, you go straight on to the lemonade."

"Yes, matron."

"You get worse." Dominic groaned.

The talk of Chough's Nest had given Morgan an idea. "We'll go and see if Harry's in the Sea Bell. Tell him what we've found. What you've found," he corrected himself, although this felt like a joint venture now, and Morgan was happy to take the credit vicariously. "He'd like that."

"Excellent idea. I need to top up my beer levels—that stuff never tastes the same from a bottle."

"I'll give him a ring." Funny how the reluctance to contact Harry had also faded away. The bridge had been crossed.

CHAPTER FOURTEEN

arry was delighted to hear from Morgan, and it came as no
surprise when he suggested meeting at the Sea Bell, about
which nobody was going to complain. Morgan didn't mention that
he'd been unwell, just warned Harry not to lead him astray as he was
going light on the sauce at present.

By the time they reached the pub, the little car park was crammed,
probably because the rain showed no sign of relenting. Rather than
trying to squeeze Dominic's car into half a space, they parked up
the road and huddled under a large umbrella which Morgan had
remembered to put in the boot. They were only a bit damp when they
fell in through the door of the bar, glad to have escaped when they'd
seen another poor sod get soaked by a car which had sped through a
puddle.

"Don't be smug," Dominic said as he shook the brolly and put it
into a stand. "Karma will come and get us, mark my words."

Morgan flung the drips off the arm of his coat. "I know. But did
you see his face?"

"Whose face?" Harry asked as he came up behind them.

"Some poor grockle who got too near to a puddle at the point a
Chelsea tractor came through it. We were smug because it wasn't us,
and Dominic reckons we'll pay for it."

Harry grinned. "Why not head it off at the pass by paying for my
beer instead?"

"Deal." Then Morgan could make sure he only had a half rather
than Harry converting it to a pint. He got the drinks in, taking them to
Harry's favourite table, where he and Dominic were already ensconced
with a pile of paper, deep in discussion about Mary Lusmoore.

"Thanks," they said, taking their beer as Morgan laid it on the table, well away from Dominic's documents.

"Fascinating stuff, this." Harry pointed at the papers with his beer-free hand. "I'd always wondered if those old stories were a load of old tripe. Not that I was going to dash your hopes last time you were here, but things do grow in the telling. Glad to see there's a grain of truth in them."

"It's the size of that grain that bothers us." Dominic took a long, languid drink of beer. "At least the grain in this never disappoints."

"Are his jokes always that bad?" Harry asked Morgan, with a roll of his eyes.

"Worse, usually." Morgan sipped at his pint; easy did it until he knew what effect the alcohol would have on his slowly recovering sense of balance. He listened while Dominic finished explaining what the last few days had turned up, avoiding—thank God—any mention of Morgan's illness.

Harry nodded at the account, chipping in with questions here and there to clarify things, demonstrating a real enthusiasm and not a polite interest.

"Right," he said, as Dominic completed their theories about the ballad. "That all makes sense. Nothing contradicts anything else."

"No, it all hangs together beautifully. Maybe too beautifully for my sceptic mind." Dominic stared into his glass, as though the true story of Midshipman Lawson and who killed him might be lurking at the bottom.

"Pessimism to go with the bad jokes." Harry smiled indulgently. "Clown who wants to play Hamlet?"

"Lay off, Harry." Morgan grinned, but he felt suddenly very protective of his lover. "If you start to think the story through, bits don't hang together. Why didn't Lawson's family come and look for him? Why didn't he try to get away?"

"You're thinking about this with a twenty-first-century mind. Do something these days and it's all over Twitter and halfway around the world in minutes. Things didn't work like that back then, and if you wanted to hide away, or keep something hidden, it was a damn sight easier." Harry turned to Dominic. "Am I right or am I right?"

"You're right," Dominic agreed. "Although 'news' can't be relied on these days, and the same would have applied when they painted those pictures of the wreck and managed to get the ship details wrong."

"That's always been the way." Harry twirled his empty glass. "Take *The Fighting Temeraire*. That's supposed to be inaccurate, as well."

"She wouldn't have had masts." Dominic nodded. "Not en route to be broken up."

Harry gave Morgan a wink. "He knows his stuff, doesn't he?"

"Regular encyclopaedia when it comes to ships." And when it came to making the best use of a double bed, but he wasn't going to tell Harry that. "And if it hadn't been for *Troilus*, he'd never have come down here and we'd have had to find someone else to annoy us."

"Funny how that there ship keeps connecting itself with your family." The sudden serious edge in Harry's voice should have been a warning, Morgan realised afterwards.

"How's that?" he asked.

Harry paused, before tapping Morgan's arm and wondering aloud, "Did your mother never mention anything to you about her dreams?"

The question sent a sickening jolt up Morgan's spine. He took a steadying swig of beer and then forced out a reply. "No."

Dominic stealthily moved nearer, subtly closing ranks.

"She used to have nightmares about the ship going down, poor lass." Harry rubbed his chin. "She said they felt horribly real, even though she was half expecting them, as her mother had similar. They saw the storm, the ship going down, like they were watching it on the telly."

Morgan couldn't answer, dumbstruck.

"Sorry, I shouldn't have mentioned it," Harry continued, hastily. "I forget how hard this business with her has hit you. You don't want to listen to an old man's scary stories. I'm a daft bugger, and you should go and forget I said anything at all."

"That's all right." Best to let Harry carry on thinking Morgan's reaction was about his mother's state of mind and not his own. He edged closer to Dominic, soaking up his presence like an anxiolytic. "We should have talked about her before now. My fault to have taken so long to get in contact again."

"No. I've been as bad, avoiding you. All mended now, though." Harry reached out to shake his hand. "You mustn't blame yourself about what happened to her. Not for any of it. I knew her mother, as well—early memory loss runs in your distaff line. Couldn't have been helped, not if you'd been the angel Gabriel himself."

"He's right." Dominic's eyes pleaded for Morgan not to get upset.

"Yeah. Like you said earlier, he's always right." Morgan managed a smile he couldn't match inside.

Outside, the skies had cleared once more, the clouds scudding off to plague Devon and Dorset, leaving blazing sunshine in their wake, but Morgan's spirits were unlikely to make a similar U-turn.

"Are you all right?" Dominic asked, as they left the pub.

"Never been better," Morgan snapped, staggering off along the street on legs that felt like jelly.

"Car's the other way," Dominic shouted after him.

"Don't care. I don't feel like going home at the moment." He heard quickening footsteps behind him, as Dominic caught up and took his arm.

"Steady on, there. You're all over the place. Are you dizzy?"

"No." Morgan wrested his arm from Dominic's grip. "Leave off."

"Hey." Dominic grabbed at him again. "Slow down. I'm worried enough about going back home and you being taken ill again."

The link to Morgan's mother having her fall when *he* had been in London did nothing to improve his mood. "You're not my keeper," he said with a scowl, picking up the pace.

"Maybe I'm not. But I'm your friend." Dominic scurried to keep in step. "What *is* the matter?"

Morgan halted suddenly, spinning on his heel and almost losing his balance in the process—not that he was going to admit it. "The matter? Don't pretend it didn't happen."

Dominic's face was infuriatingly blank. "What didn't happen?"

"Harry talking about Mum's nightmares. You heard what he said. She had the same dream as I did." A convenient fence post took the brunt of Morgan's wrath as he kicked out at it. The contact hurt, but not as much as the tight knot in his stomach. "So did Gran, and I bet *her* mother did as well. The first sign that they were losing their minds."

"You don't know that." Dominic shook his head. "You're drawing conclusions where there are none."

"Don't be stupid. That's a hell of a coincidence otherwise." He drew back his foot to kick the post again, then stopped; he was beginning to frighten himself. "Don't keep playing everything down. Please. It doesn't help me."

"I'm simply trying to put things into perspective. If your family have been telling and retelling stories about that wreck and those beams since the night the ship sank, then maybe they've been firing up other imaginations." Dominic grabbed at Morgan's arm again. "Odd things happen to people under strain, and you've been under a lot of it. Everybody gets bad dreams."

"Yeah, but they're not all losing their marbles." Morgan put his hands to his face, lost in a welter of emotions.

"Just hear me out. Please."

Morgan opened his mouth, then simply nodded. "Not in public, though." This needed to be a private torture. He crossed the road to where a small, semi-derelict chapel set back from the road was evidently awaiting somebody converting it into a des res.

They perched on the garden wall, away from the pavement and out of view of the pub door, in case Harry came out; Morgan couldn't face him too, not in this mood. "Go on. I'm listening."

Dominic took a deep breath. "For a start, dementia seems to run in the female line of your family. You're a bloke."

"Yeah, but the blokes in our family have a habit of not living long enough to find out whether they'll get dementia." That's why Morgan didn't smoke, and kept an eye on his weight—he could guard against heart disease. He crossed his arms over his stomach, trying to quell the nausea. "And that 'female line' bit doesn't explain why I had the same dream as Mum and Gran."

"There could be a reasonable explanation." Dominic raised his hand to brook any argument. "No, please listen. What if your mother told you about that dream, when you were little? The same way she must have told Harry."

Morgan wanted to believe that, but some cussed part of him refused to be mollified. "I don't remember that happening. Surely I would have done, back when I first had my nightmare and was trying to find an explanation."

"Maybe you don't consciously remember, but your subconscious does. Maybe you were very young, or you only overheard her telling Harry and didn't really register what you were hearing."

It was a reasonable explanation.

"Then that memory reappeared in the dream you had. That makes a lot more sense than you dreaming about the stories you heard at your granny's knee. It would be like your mother's dream because you'd replayed exactly what you heard."

That was possible; it gave Morgan a straw to clutch at, although he wasn't convinced it was the truth. "I can't prove that though, can I? I wouldn't be able to get a sensible answer from Mum, even if I felt like asking her, which I'm reluctant to do. It might finish her off completely reminding her of something she found so disturbing."

"Would your brother know?"

"I'm not asking *him*." That had pressed all the wrong buttons. Morgan jumped off the wall, to pace up and down the patchy grass in front of the chapel, trying to calm down. "He doesn't understand about things if they don't make money."

Dominic shifted his position. "Isn't that a bit harsh?"

"You haven't met him and his wife. Unless James has been telling you all about *them* too."

"What *are* you going on about? Where does James come into any of this? What *is* eating you?"

"Can you stop this?" Morgan shouted.

Dominic flinched, his voice taking on a deliberately soothing tone, like he might have used with a fractious child. "I thought I'd been helping you. You said it was good to talk."

"It is and it isn't. I don't know." Morgan stopped his pacing, hands clenching and unclenching. "Maybe our talking is making it worse. Papering over the cracks."

"Then get some proper help, like I keep telling you to. If you're that worried about it, then see an expert." Dominic, pale and shaking, drummed his fingers against his thighs.

"I could do that," Morgan snapped, "if you'd give me some space to get my mind clear."

"If you want space, I'll go." Dominic muttered.

"What was that?"

"I said I'll go. Right now." Dominic reached into his pocket, fishing out the keys to his hire car in trembling hands. "Just give me time to pack my stuff from the house into the car boot and I'll be out of your hair. I may not be able to find a hotel for tonight, but I'd rather sleep on the backseat than stay where I'm not wanted."

"Do it, then." Morgan kicked at a stone. "That works for me."

"I don't give a flying fuck whether it works for you or not." Dominic had never displayed such anger; was that his true colours coming out?

Morgan jabbed his finger repeatedly in Dominic's direction. "If that's the way you feel, why bother to run me home? I can get a taxi back to Cadoc. You can go ahead, take my door key and leave it under the flowerpot."

"Don't be so bloody ridiculous. You'll do no such thing. I'm not having my conscience kicking me if you're taken ill again. Anyway, the sooner I get you home, the sooner you can be rid of me."

Morgan opened his mouth, snapped it shut again, then turned on his heel, heading back to the car park. He didn't want to talk to Dominic, didn't want to see his face, for that matter. The journey home was going to be agony, but better to go through it now, and make a clean break as soon as possible. Better for all concerned.

"Morgan . . ."

He ignored the pleading voice.

"Morgan, please."

"Will you stop it, okay?" He kept his eyes fixed ahead. "We've got nothing left to say to each other." From the hush that ensued behind him, Morgan guessed he'd made his point.

When they got to the car, Morgan got into one of the rear passenger seats, and Dominic didn't argue about it. Staring out of the car window in silence was preferable to having Dominic's face within sight, the pair of them trying not to catch each other's gaze. If his guest turned on *that* smile, Morgan risked weakening, just when he was seeing things plainly. He'd been so tired the last few days, so confused, but the conversation with Harry—shock and all—had shone a terrible light on matters.

It wasn't only, if at all, about Dominic's platitudes or his failing to understand how scared *he* was, how that fear couldn't be sent away with any amount of touchy-feely crap. Those excuses felt increasingly like something he'd grabbed at on the spur of the moment, to cover over the real reason he wanted Dominic to go. If Morgan was going to slide down the same slope as his mother—and that seemed increasingly like a possibility—he didn't want to take anybody on the ride with him.

He wouldn't inflict on anyone else the same pain he'd suffered with her, especially not somebody he'd come to value as much as he did Dominic.

By the time they reached the house, Morgan had broken the painful silence, but only by swearing at a cyclist who'd been swerving all over the road and nearly taken the wing mirror off. Dominic had joined in the stream of invective, evidently relieved that he'd been called back from Coventry. Dominic parked the car, but before he had the chance to get out, Morgan leaned forward to speak.

"I know we're not supposed to apologise, but I'm saying sorry. About earlier. I didn't mean to be so aggressive. To use a bloody awful cliché, it's not you, it's me." As Morgan spoke the words, James's letter flashed through his mind. He was doing to another undeserving soul exactly what the rat had done to him, but it couldn't be helped. "I'm not myself, and I need some space to get my head clear. It's all getting too much."

"So is that simply a politer way of telling me to bugger off and not come back than the last one you tried?" Dominic's voice was angry, upset, brave, all at once. Morgan focussed on the hand brake, avoiding the bloke's gaze in the rearview mirror.

"No." He almost believed the lie. "I can't think straight. I want to see what the next few months bring and work out how to deal with it on my own." How pathetic did he sound?

"But you know what's going to happen. You'll get yourself screwed up without somebody to help you through."

"Don't tell me what to do. You don't run my life. You're not—"
He'd nearly said, he realised with a jolt to his stomach, *my mother*.
"Anyway, I don't need to explain. I need a bit of space. Please let me
have it."

He should just get out of the car, unlock the front door, and wait
for Dominic to take up his bags and walk. Only he couldn't move.
He had to have an answer, although none seemed to be coming other
than Dominic's steady breathing. Morgan's patience wasn't infinite,
so he opened the car door and eased himself out all in one careful
movement.

"Okay, I'm going." Dominic followed Morgan along the path to
the house. "For the moment."

Morgan pretended not to hear the last bit.

"You've got my number," Dominic continued. "If you change
your mind, you can call. I'll always be there, if you need me.
When you've had your space or whatever."

That had to get a reply. Morgan stopped by the front door, as he
slid his key into the Chubb lock, but all he could manage was, "Okay."

Dominic nodded, then waited in silence As Morgan opened the
door and stood to one side. They'd said all they had to say.

Later, as Morgan—once again—watched his guest drive away,
the sound of blowing up bridges filled his mind's ears. Arguments
didn't have to mean the end of things—he and James had argued
often, making up again in a flurry of apologies, mainly from Morgan's
side—but that had been different. In this case, he didn't even know if
he wanted to resolve things.

And that was the problem in a nutshell. What *did* he want? And
what the hell was he going to do now?

CHAPTER
FIFTEEN

Wednesday dawned grey and misty, although not as foggy as the contents of Morgan's head. How many had he put away the evening before? Too many, judging by the headache and the empty bottles on the kitchen drainer. It was a surprise he hadn't had another attack of vertigo as he'd staggered from his bedroom this morning, bleary-eyed and none too steady on his feet.

Had Dominic also taken refuge in beer? Morgan didn't want to think about Dominic, given the hole he'd left behind him in both heart and bed.

Morgan had work to do, but couldn't face it, and he didn't fancy going out anywhere given the state of the weather, much less the state of his mind and his inner ears. The thing that nagged him most was the need to see his mother, irrespective of what the nursing home sister had said about staying away until he was well. For once his motive wasn't guilt; although whether he primarily wanted to ask her about the ship dream or grab some crumb of comfort—reassure himself that somebody still loved him—he wasn't sure.

He *wouldn't* check his phone to see if Dominic had texted. He *wouldn't* check his inbox for a message from the bloke. He'd made his bed, and he was going to have to lie in it, empty or not.

Morgan managed to get to lunchtime using the same technique he'd used after James's Dear John letter. Get through ten minutes, then another ten. *Don't think about ships or nightmares or Dominic, no matter how much they want to invade your mind. Don't think about living the rest of your life on your own.* He ate a lunch, of sorts, not having been able to face anything other than water and a plain cracker at breakfast, and the cracker had only been to line his stomach before he took two ibuprofen.

The roads to the nursing home were half-term busy, but for once Morgan didn't mind, glad to be taking it slowly in case he got dizzy again, and also grateful for something to help fill the interminable day. The car felt empty without Dominic by his side; strange how the bloke had so quickly got himself under Morgan's skin, so soon become part of the fabric of his everyday life. Morgan stared at the traffic ahead.

Don't think about Dominic.

Once he was through the doors of the nursing home, his favourite nurse greeted him with a cheery smile. A pretty, capable girl, with a deep West Indian accent and an unflappable air about her, she exuded calm—spending time in her presence soothed patients and visitors alike.

"Good afternoon, Christine."

"Hello, Mr. Capell. You've brought the sunshine with you."

"I try my best." Morgan smiled. "Glad that sea fog burned off. How's Mum today?"

"She's having quite a good day. Sitting out in the garden clicking away merrily."

"Clicking?"

"Her knitting."

"Oh, yes. Sorry. Being thick."

"You're allowed." The nurse smiled and let him get on.

Morgan found his mother seated in her favourite part of the garden, creating something fluffy out of white wool. He couldn't remember the last time she'd concentrated so intently on a task.

"Hi, Mum." He waved as he strolled along the path that weaved through spring-bright flower beds.

"Hello, love. Come and sit here, in the sun."

"What are you making?"

She held up the fruits of her labours. "It's a matinee jacket. One of the nurses here is expecting her first grandchild."

It wasn't the best matinee jacket he'd ever seen, but he nodded enthusiastically. She'd clearly retained some of her skills. "It'll be lovely. You carry on with it while we chat."

"You used to do that when you were a boy. Natter away as I knitted."

"I remember." Maybe the familiar, repeated movements of her fingers were refiring neurons somewhere in her mind, triggering memories that had long lain dormant. They chatted calmly about a favourite scarf she'd made for him when he was nine, how he'd worn it all one winter until it had been so disgusting she'd had to steal it from him so it could be washed. How it had never quite been the same soft, comforting item again, and he'd been in a right temper about it.

"You always were a changeable boy. One minute bright as the sun and the next moody as anything." She tapped his arm before setting about another row of stitches.

"Was I?" Then nothing had changed.

"Oh, yes. Like your pal Derek."

"Derek?"

"The one with the feckless mother. Remember his jumper?"

"I do. She put his favourite sweater in their new washing machine, and it came out half the size." Morgan grinned in recollection.

His mother giggled. "He was that upset, wasn't he? How we laughed about it later."

Derek still laughed about it now, on the occasions they ran into each other at the pub. Morgan would have to remember to tell him what she'd said; he'd always got on well with Mum. "He had a great big teddy bear, remember? Mr. Smudge. He put the jumper on it. His kids play with it now—right beaten-up old thing it is—but he won't have it any other way."

"He always was daft." She finished her row, concentrating on the stitches. "Him and his pirate captains. The pair of you dashing round the garden, pretending you were brave."

"Oh yes. I'd forgotten." Derek had gone through a phase where everything was *Ooh aar!* and *Avast me hearties*, not that either of them knew what *avast* meant. Even Mr. Smudge had been made to wear an eye patch. Talking of pirates, albeit teddy bear ones, provided an unexpected opportunity to broach the subject of ships. "I wonder if *he* dreamed about shipwrecks?"

"I beg your pardon?" She looked up from her knitting.

"I wonder if Derek dreamed about shipwrecks, seeing as he was so mad on pirates. I once had a nightmare about a ship sinking."

"Did you, love?" She laid her needles down in her lap. "That's funny. I think I used to dream about the same thing. It was horrible."

"I bet it was. Can you remember anything about it? Some of the details?"

"I don't know. I think the ship got driven onto the rocks, but . . ." Voice faltering, she dropped her knitting entirely and grabbed hold of Morgan's arm. "I can't remember, Morgan. Why can't I? What's happening to me?"

"It's all right." He patted her hand, unsure of what to do. She'd not had one of these panic attacks for a long time: the first had been heartbreaking to deal with and this was hardly any easier.

Christine appeared from the open French doors, probably alerted by raised voices and agitated tones. She came over, making soothing noises. "There, there. How's the knitting going, Ruth? It's coming along lovely."

Morgan's mother held the matinee jacket up, staring at it blankly.

"She got a bit upset," Morgan explained. The words were inadequate to the situation, as any might have been; he felt another wave of vulnerability assail him.

"Who's that?" Mum laid down her knitting and jabbed a bony finger at the nurse. "Why am I being kept here? Why can't I go home?"

"It's Christine. You like her."

The nurse pulled up a chair beside Morgan's mother, patting her hand and making the inconsequential small talk they always used at the home when one of the residents became fractious. Morgan might as well have not been present, but he was determined to stay this time; he had questions to ask.

Eventually his mother settled again, taking up her knitting and ploughing on with it in silence. Christine rose, motioning for Morgan to follow her; he kissed his mum's head, then did as instructed.

"Don't upset yourself," Christine said, once they were out of earshot. "It happens. She'll be right as rain in a while. Or at least as right as we can hope for."

"Thank you. For calming Mum down." Morgan steadied himself with a deep breath. "Can I ask you something that's going to sound odd?"

"Of course. Let's go inside." She led him into the conservatory, where they could watch his mother but not be seen by her. Mum's mood seemed to have regained its former equilibrium as she chatted and sang to herself over her knitting, much as she'd always done.

"She seems happy again."

Christine nodded. "She has her ups and downs every day, the way we all do. Although for her they're exaggerated."

"She was so placid at home. Before all this happened. She's like a different person."

"Yes. It's hard seeing somebody you know change so greatly, but she's fine here, honestly. We can deal with her needs much better than you could. Don't feel guilty about it."

"Am I that obvious?" Morgan had to smile. This was a conversation he should have had long ago, but there'd not been anybody who felt trustworthy enough—and far enough removed—to have it with. Harry was too close and Dominic . . . he was too valued. Now he was certain he couldn't put Dominic through the same agony of guilt and distress.

"In my experience, it's rare that anyone commits their parents into care without blaming themselves for not having done enough to help them. To keep them at home." The nurse patted his arm, as though he was one of her charges. "She'd never be able to cope outside of residential care, not even in sheltered accommodation. Not without somebody's eye on her all the time. For most families, that twenty-four-hour pair of eyes isn't an option."

"It could have been an option, for me. I work from home. I could have had the house adapted or something."

"You could. And you might have been able to afford a nurse to come in to cover the times you couldn't. If you were lucky, it might have worked out fine. Chances are she'd have become a growing worry to you. And a burden." Christine's voice became increasingly reassuring; she must have had this conversation many times. "You might have ended up hating your mother. We're none of us saints."

She was right. Despite working from home, Morgan wouldn't have had his mother continually in his sight. She could have easily gone wandering, as had happened to an elderly neighbour of theirs twenty years ago. *He'd* managed to get out of a house which the family had believed secure, only to end up lunging himself out onto the main road, where a car hadn't been able to avoid hitting him. How much guiltier would Morgan have felt under those circumstances?

"You visit her regularly, and she's pleased to see you," Christine continued. "It's more than some people do. She often talks about you."

"Does she?"

"Of course, although usually it's as though you were still a little boy. Maybe that's what you'll always be in her mind."

"It seems like it." Morgan steadied himself with a deep breath. "Does she ever mention ships at all? Or a nightmare she once had about a ship? That's what I was talking about when she got upset. I don't want to ask her again in case it sets her off."

Christine produced an unreadable smile. "Is it important?"

"Yes. Very. This is going to seem really stupid, but that dream seems to recur in our family, and I wanted to know when she had it and how often." It did seem stupid, described in such stark terms, but how could anybody understand its significance if they hadn't experienced the thing?

"It's strange you should mention it. She's spoken about that dream to me a few times. At first we thought she'd had the nightmare here, something to do with her medication or her mental state, but she's adamant it happened when you were still young. That part of the story never changes."

"What about the details of the dream? Are they always the same?" Morgan raised his hand. "Yes, I know, please bear with me. It's an odd question, but I can promise you I wouldn't ask if it didn't matter."

"Okay." Shrugging, Christine smiled. "It's the same story every time she talks about it. Which is odd, because she's obviously not consistent about other things in her life. Apart from your dad's old boss. She never changes the story about *her*."

Morgan grinned. "Miss Charlton. When I was young, I used to imagine her as a real live dragon, blowing fire out of her nostrils. I suppose she was a bit modern for mum's tastes."

"If she'd been a Mr. Charlton and done the same things, it wouldn't have been such a problem, I guess." Christine laughed.

"Something like that." At least Miss Charlton would never have been a rival for Dad's affections. Morgan had recognised her likely inclinations as he'd gone through the process of understanding his own sexuality. "Sorry to harp on about this dream, but what does Mum say happens in it?"

"Oh, apparently it's all very vivid, like something out of a film. A storm and a shipwreck, out on some rocks called . . ." Christine wrinkled her brow in thought. "The devil's anchor?"

"The Devil's Anvil."

"Yes, that's it. Such a horrible name. Is it a real place?"

"I'm afraid it's all too real. As was the wreck. A ship called *Troilus*." He had to force himself to speak the name, a feat he'd not had a problem with in what seemed an age.

Christine nodded, clearly impressed that another aspect of her patient's story was correct, and seemingly unaware of Morgan's discomfort. "Oh yes? I'm afraid I don't know all the tales from round here. Maybe when I've been here long enough to be called a local, I'll have a better idea."

"You could live here fifty years and still be counted as a visitor, I'm afraid." Morgan shook his head, ruefully. "No matter how well you knew the legends. Can you remember anything else she said about that dream?"

"Not really. Except that all the sailors were drowned except one who got washed up on the beach. Quite a story! She must have a powerful imagination."

"She has. Storytelling runs in the family. That's why I'm trying to pick apart the truth from any embellishment that might have happened along the way. I've had a similar nightmare, you see," Morgan continued, in response to the nurse's quizzical look.

"Ah, I see. How peculiar." The crucifix that Christine wore round her neck—and the odd remark she'd dropped in the past about her faith—suggested she might have no time for a paranormal explanation.

"Yes. And from what you've said, it doesn't simply sound similar. It's almost exactly the same." Except in his version there weren't survivors. What the hell did that signify?

"Now that's something." Christine tapped the arm of her chair, theatrically. "Your mother was telling me that *her* mother had the same dream, about the same ship. And her mother before her. We didn't believe such a thing could be true—the ladies here tell us the most amazing stories, so we've learned to take them all with a pinch of salt—but it seems we were wrong."

"Sad to say, you were." Morgan shivered, despite the warmth of the conservatory. "I had no idea she'd had that dream, not until yesterday, when a friend of the family mentioned Mother had told him about it. I thought it had only happened to me."

"Maybe that nightmare runs in your family alongside the storytelling. Or because of it. You heard about your mother's dream when you were too young to remember it, but it stuck somewhere in your brain. Like with her." Christine tipped her head in the direction of his mother, who'd laid down her knitting and was slumbering peacefully. "Memories must be still in her brain somewhere, but they don't come out in the right order or at the right time."

"Hm. Maybe."

"You don't think that's the explanation?"

"I have no idea. A . . . a friend suggested something similar, but it doesn't ring true."

"Why not? It seems the simplest explanation, rather than any old mumbo-jumbo." She snorted. "What did your mother say when you had your nightmare?"

"Nothing. I mean, only the normal comfort for someone who's had a bad dream. I didn't want to go into the details at the time—I was young and scared, and I couldn't think logically." He wasn't thinking a lot more logically as an adult. "I wish now I had spoken about it. Maybe I'd be able to understand what's going on. But she clearly didn't want to tell *me* about *her* dream, did she? Despite telling Harry."

"Harry?"

"That friend I mentioned."

"Ah." Christine nodded again. "She must have been protecting you, in case you started worrying too much. Are you a worrier?"

Morgan had to laugh. "Guilty as charged. Although maybe I'm worrying about it because I *don't* know."

"Then nobody could win with you, could they?" Christine eased out of her chair, Morgan following suit. "I'm afraid I have jobs to do. Sorry I couldn't be of further help."

"You've helped a lot, honestly." At least to clarify things if not to make them better. "And thanks for all you do with Mum. You connect with her when I can't."

"That's years of practice." She peered out into the garden again. "Go and kiss her before you leave. Don't wake her if you don't want to. She's happy for the moment, and we should be grateful for these times."

"We should. I'll try to be." Morgan fiddled in his pockets. "Thank you. For listening to me. It helps."

"No worries." Christine patted his arm. "See you again soon."

"Yep. I'm like the proverbial bad penny. Always turning up." He took a final look at his mother; he'd go and give her that kiss, careful not to wake her when she seemed so content, in case it upset her again.

Once in his car, he stared at the steering wheel, unseeing and with that tight knot of pain back in his stomach, turning over the conversation in his mind. If his mother's account could be trusted, the thing he'd dreaded—that all the women who'd become prematurely senile had experienced the same nightmare—appeared to be true.

So where did that leave him?

Back at the house, Morgan wandered into the kitchen, wandered out again, went into the lounge, decided to flick on the telly, but couldn't settle. Not even the schadenfreude engendered by the travel news and the thought of all the grockles stuck in traffic jams made him feel any better. He was at the loosest of loose ends, hovering at the point where he needed to occupy his brain with something other than dread, and stop him hitting another bottle or six of beer. Getting smashed the night before had done no harm to his balance, but he might not be so lucky next time.

That reminded him about his upcoming appointment with his GP; he saw no reason now why he should keep his promise to Dominic to go through with it, but he guessed he owed it to himself. Either his worst fears might be justified, or his mind could be put at rest, although the thought of the first outcome made him feel physically sick. That bloody dream had blighted his life for so long, and it seemed determined to keep on blighting it.

He stretched out on the settee, flicking onto an old episode of *Poirot*, and settled down for a doze. He didn't need to make a decision about seeing the doctor until the day itself.

The unmistakable sound of a bosun's whistle followed by a broadside going off roused him from sleep in a cold sweat. Had he been having the nightmare again, somehow without being aware of it? His relief of seeing that yet another repeat of *Hornblower* was being aired, following on from the murder mystery, was unbelievable. He turned the television off, not wanting to be reminded of ships, then went to make a cup of tea, although he couldn't keep his thoughts away from Midshipman Lawson and Mary Lusmoore.

As he caught sight of the family picture on the wall, a flood of memories returned. *Dad was interested in local history. He did all that stuff on Porthkennack bloodlines, remember?* Morgan could recite the names: the Edes, the Quicks, the Roscarrocks, and all the rest, from the highly respectable to those you wouldn't want to meet in a dark alley. Most of them had lived in the area since Noah came out of the ark, preserving the family genome away from outside influence.

Why couldn't he have remembered his dad's hobby sooner? Instead of legging it all round Porthkennack in search of the Lusmoores, they might have been able to turn something up in this very house. Was that oversight further evidence of Morgan losing it?

He'd try not to pursue that line of thought, not in the bleak mental state he already inhabited. He should do something practical; maybe poking about in the stuff his dad had left would be exactly the mindless pastime he was in need of.

And while Morgan couldn't remember his father mentioning the Lusmoores as one of his targets, it was entirely possible he'd been on their trail, at least peripherally. All the old local families were interconnected. The only stumbling block was locating the research itself, because Morgan wasn't sure where all Dad's material had gone after his death.

He remembered having to go up into the loft to root out that stash of money his mother had told him about. There'd been a load of other stuff up there, mainly the typical debris of old carpets, suitcases, boxes, and the like. What if Dad's old books and papers had been stuffed away up there? Not only would going through them give Morgan something positive to concentrate on, but clearing that old rubbish while he was about it would make him feel better. Nothing like slinging out a pile of physical crap to make the emotional crap sit more easily.

The loft proved pleasantly cool on an afternoon that had turned horribly clammy; unless the sweatiness of Morgan's palms came from the state he was in. The electric light was bright enough to see but not read by, so the torch Morgan had taken up with him would be invaluable. The first suitcase he opened contained nothing but old clothes, possibly his grandparents'. That could go straight out to a charity shop or the local welfare project, preferably tomorrow morning, so it didn't hang around making him think of his grandmother.

The second case was empty, apart from a collection of insects which had wormed their way in, as was the third. They'd be best sent straight to the dump, while he was en route to the charity shop—his thoughts turned to bats or deathwatch beetles and the many other nasty things he could find hidden away in forgotten places. He shone his torch up at the roof beams, but they seemed to be a flying-mammal-free zone.

The old handbag he'd found his mother's stash of money in lay next to some old packing crates, but he wasn't too eager to dispose of that bag while she was still alive; he couldn't be that heartless. The packing crates themselves could be hopeful, though. The first was half filled with books, which was unusual given that there were several bookshelves round the house with gaps on them, so lack of storage space couldn't have been the reason these volumes had been consigned to the loft. The most obvious explanation seemed to be that they were related to the serial hobbies Dad had indulged in, and been put away when his interest had changed. With a pang of sadness, Morgan found a history of the church he and Dominic had visited, probably the same book the bloke had been shown by the verger. After staring at it blankly, thinking of some old song about having something and losing it going through his mind, he placed the book carefully to one side of the stuff he was getting rid of. He could decide what to do with it later.

The second crate had no lid, only an old curtain laid across it, but on lifting it, he seemed to have struck gold. Dusty, dirty ring binders, a whole colony of them, all full of neatly filed, ring-reinforced pieces of paper. Paper which, on inspection, bore the unmistakably spidery handwriting of his father. Each binder was marked up with the name of one of the usual suspects—Ede, Roscarrock, all the boys in the band. If he really had struck gold, there'd be a Lusmoore file somewhere, and minutes later, in what felt an inevitable course of events, it turned up right at the bottom of the box, just as he was giving up hope.

Morgan pored through the pages, some sticking together due to the weight of the other families' histories. He felt the same, crushed under the weight of stories and experiences, unable to pick apart the important from the irrelevant. Time to get back to his dad's researches.

There was a fair amount of stuff that was no use to him, being far too recent in the Lusmoore timeline, but a large piece of yellowed paper, meticulously folded, caught his eye. A family tree, neatly written in old-fashioned ink, showed the line of the Lusmoores going back to where he wanted it. There was Mary and her parents: she was shown as being without husband or issue, although a pencilled-in question mark next to her name and something else next to that, indecipherable in this light, intrigued him.

If there was something about the Lusmoores, was there also something to be found about Lawson? He put the paper back in the file, preparatory to taking it downstairs for a proper going over.

Before doing that, he checked the other two packing cases: one contained nothing but watercolour painting stuff—Dad's previous interest before getting the family-history bug—and the second seemed equally unpromising, being half full of football and theatre programmes. Morgan turned the top layer over, then realised the collection was much more eclectic. Among the souvenirs from Wembley and the London Palladium were tourist guides, local interest books, and oddities, like a brochure from Porthkennack's celebration of the queen's coronation. Should he keep them or add them to the pile of stuff for charity? The Oxfam bookshop liked to sell this type of stuff, but would making these breaks with the past make him feel any better or simply add to his burden of guilt?

Decisive for once, he tipped them out and began to sort, in case there was a gem among the dross. Among the old tourist guides and local interest books was a small, evidently self-published pamphlet by a Reverend George Morrison. It was dog-eared and faded, but the title was plain enough to read despite the dim light—*The Unlucky Midshipman: a story of imprudent love and heinous treachery*. That title, with the dramatic and likely inaccurate etching of a young ship's officer below it on the cover, made Morgan grin. If Dominic were to write a book, he'd probably call it something similarly archaic and pompous.

Dominic. After all those bloody hours and days of trying not to think of James; now he'd got to stop thinking of *him*. Although wasn't rummaging about in search of a midshipman—*their* midshipman as Morgan had so fatefully referred to him that evening they went out for a meal—keeping Dominic right in the forefront of his mind?

He packed the leaflet up inside the Lusmoore file, dumped the rest of the stuff back in the box, jumbling it all up again, then took his trophies downstairs, unsettled and no longer able to take pleasure in his rummaging. If it turned out he *had* found something relevant to Lawson, would he let Dominic know or would he sit smugly on the information, trying to keep his indignation warm? An indignation that had become decidedly tepid, anyway? If there was anybody he should be cross at, it was himself, for being such a bloody idiot all round.

That bottle of wine was calling, and a glass wouldn't hurt so long as he resisted the temptation to put the whole bottle away. Maybe it would clear his head, hair of the dog and all that, although probably best to grab something to eat first. He transferred an instant meal from freezer to microwave, then laid a tray of cutlery and crockery on autopilot, trying not to think of how bleak such an always-catering-for-one existence would be for him if it became permanent.

He gazed out of the kitchen window, catching a glimpse of the Devil's Anvil, the rocks appearing to form a great jagged smile to taunt him. Sod the rocks. Sod ships. Sod everything. He turned his back and got on with making his dinner, because that seemed about the only worthwhile thing he had to do at present.

CHAPTER SIXTEEN

Aplate of food and a glass of wine later, his mood hadn't improved. He'd had another dizzy spell, not as bad as the one in the graveyard but enough to remind him that he was still on the road to recovery and claret wasn't helping.

Then the ridiculous oversight about his father's family-history research started nagging at him, upsetting him more than the story of the recurring dream. How long was it going to be before he became so forgetful he ended up like his mother, barely able to organise his thoughts? Thank God it was likely she'd be gone by the time he turned completely gaga.

He contemplated the pile of stuff from the loft, had a "what's the bloody point?" moment before deciding he might as well sort it, because he couldn't face work at the moment and didn't have anything else pressing to occupy himself with. Except the bottle of wine and that would only make him feel worse. He had to fetch an old rag to go over the hoard; he hadn't realised in the poor light up there just how filthy and flyblown the books were. He flicked in a desultory way through the book about the church, but there was nothing he hadn't seen in Dominic's photocopy.

The Lusmoore timeline proved intriguing. The pencilled scribble next to Mary's name looked like it read *Lawson* followed by something else, although that might have been wishful thinking. It could equally have been "laundry" or any other of a dozen words. But when he took the document over to peruse in the better light from the standard lamp, his dad's familiar handwriting, which he recognised with a pang of renewed sorrow, was plain.

Lawson. No grave. The note in his fingers began shaking—Morgan steadied both it and his hand against the window.

See other note. Other note? Where the hell was that to be found? Dad had always kept his papers in good order, and there hadn't been anything like a random note stuffed among the contents of the crates.

Morgan crossed the room, picked up the Lusmoore file, and then shook it in order to coax out any loose pieces of paper which might have been hidden there. Nothing emerged, no matter how much he flicked the pages. If the note still existed, it was probably with the other stuff in the loft, and he had no desire to clamber back up there. He was about to shut the file, when he noticed pieces of yellowed Sellotape sticking over the top of some of the pages, attaching pictures, paper cuttings, and the like. Working through the file again, he found the note he wanted about halfway.

Lawson survived the wreck? Plenty of coincidental evidence that he did. (Local gossip, uniform, book.)

So Dad had reached the same conclusion as he and Dominic, based on the similar information. Had he found anything definitive, though?

Mary Lusmoore said to have helped save him, only to tip him over the cliff. Evidence? Ballad.

Nothing new there.

The medallion found in the rock cleft. Need to research the story.

What medallion in what rock cleft? Morgan went through the Lusmoore file again, then the book about the church, but there were no further notes, no evidence of any of these researches, if his father had ever completed them, and he hadn't lost interest when he'd moved on to his next pastime. Dominic would have a field day over that medallion story.

Only Dominic wasn't going to hear about it, was he?

Morgan put the Lusmoore stuff into a bag. Maybe he should simply parcel it all up and post it, with a businesslike note mentioning the medallion but no apology or expectation of a reply. Something cool and cursory might be a particularly effective way of bringing things between him and Dominic to an end than a continued radio silence.

Morgan recalled that conversation they'd had on the sand, about how people didn't talk to each other enough. Ironic that they should have ended up in the same position, when they seemed to have spent hours on end gassing to each other about things both trivial and important. Perhaps they'd expended all they had to say.

Or perhaps Dominic would feel the need to say sorry one final time, and would be on the phone in the morning. Morgan could imagine how such a conversation might go.

"I'm scared." He'd say. *"Apologies can't make that go away."*

"So get proper help, like I've said a dozen times."

"What's the point? It's not like a broken leg you can stick in plaster until it sets or your back, that's going to get better of its own accord. There's no cure, nothing to stop it. You either end up fading away like Mum or . . ."

"Or what?"

"You throw yourself over the cliff. Might as well make an end of it rather than turning into a vegetable."

He knew what Dominic's response to that would be. Checking if Morgan was serious—or even halfway serious. Threatening that if there was a grain of truth in what Morgan said then he'd be coming straight round, irrespective of whether he was still in Cornwall or halfway across the country. Saying he'd tie Morgan to the front door or the bed or the kitchen table until he'd talked some sense into him.

The thought of the imaginary conversation lifted his spirits more than a real one might have done at this point. Make-believe Dominic was much easier to deal with; make-believe Dominic couldn't be hurt. And if Morgan really intended throwing himself off a cliff, why didn't he get up, go off, and do it? Why live with the anguish? Was it only the thought that it might finish his mother off entirely that stopped him, or was there still some light in the darkness that wasn't a wrecker luring ships onto the rocks?

Catching sight of the pile of things he'd brought downstairs, Morgan felt again the urge to chuck the lot away. He scooped everything up, ready to consign it all to the dustbin; halfway to the kitchen, he turned so woozy he had to drop the lot and steady himself on the back of a chair. Definitely no more claret for the foreseeable future. One of the older books, spine and binding cracked and kept together by mere luck, had fragmented, and among the loose pages strewing the carpet lay a little book which had been slipped among them.

The True History of the Wreck of the Troilus: A reliable and astonishing account as told to the author by an eye witness.

Bloody hell. This book had been here all the time, as much a part of the house as the beams, and he'd had no idea. Gingerly, he picked it up, flicked through it; the title itself would date the book to the 1800s, as would the illustrations on the first few pages, one of which brought him up short. The ship depicted was nothing like the painting in the museum and everything like the one he'd seen in his nightmare, so much so he almost dropped the book. If he was going to read the text, he'd better get himself some strong coffee in lieu of alcohol.

Settled down again, mug in one hand and book in the other, Morgan began to go through the familiar story, an account that proved horribly familiar in every detail. The date, late August, was etched into his memory. The time of day—sun just setting on the horizon—and the weather—wind to the north, whipping up the grey sea into white flecks, howling through the air and rattling the windows of the local cottages—rang a bell. The Devil's Anvil awash with spray, its jagged grin hidden against the darkening sky.

Coffee splashing on his trousers from the mug that was trembling in his hands like a cat after a pigeon, reminded him how much of a shock to the system this was turning out to be. He put down his coffee mug and gingerly picked up the book again.

The account ran on, depicting events exactly as they'd been in his dream, as though *he'd* written this account rather than the anonymous early-Victorian author. Morgan read on, sweaty palmed, reliving his dream with every detail of the story. The frigate, a razee, struggling to get along the coast, decks washed with the waves and sailors hanging on for dear life to any available rope. The wind driving them onto the shore . . .

Morgan put the book down once more, reached for his coffee, then drew back, not able to trust his hands from shaking. What the hell did this mean? Was that "past life" crap going to turn out to be true, that he really had witnessed the wreck and was experiencing every detail of it in his nightmares?

He was about to get the bottle of wine and drain the lot when he realised he was being the biggest fucking idiot in the world. Nobody needed to have been around two hundred years previously to have learned all those minutiae. They'd simply have had to do what he'd done earlier—read the book, or have it read to him. The sense of relief, hard on the heels of the shock, made his head spin.

Morgan picked the book back up, reading all the way through to the end, less frightened now by the familiarity of what the text contained. There was no mention of Lawson, although the statement that all on board had *apparently* been lost gave some leeway. At the end, there were a couple of blank pages which had been written on at some point in the distant past, given how the writing had faded. Not his dad's handwriting—not a script he recognised at all—and the words were barely legible. Perhaps it was the typical "this book belongs to" statement like might get scribbled on the frontispiece, although in this instance the volume of print already there had prevented it.

He turned the page, to find a list of names. Not Capell family members, but the distaff line, each name written in a unique style, probably by the person concerned. The list started with what must have been Morgan's several times great-grandfather, given the fact the last few generations were familiar names, passing through a line of daughters, and leading to his mother. The last entry on the list staggered him afresh.

His name, scrawled in a childish hand. So he *must* have come across the book already. Had Dominic been right all the time?

There was one realistic chance of finding out—two if he included Harry, but if *he* knew about the tome, surely he'd have mentioned it. His brother, Eddie, might know something, although that begged the question about why Morgan's name was there and not his. And if this was such an important part of family history, with those names so carefully inscribed there on the page, why had it suffered the ignominy of being consigned to the loft with a load of tat? A simple phone call would clarify matters.

Only he wasn't going to ring his brother, was he? For a start, Eddie would be suspicious about what had prompted him to get in touch; for seconds, there'd be a huge risk that the story about the dreams would come about; and last—no means least—he might blurt out his worries about his mental state. Eddie hadn't shown much understanding towards Mum; Morgan wasn't giving him the chance to do the same to him. Talking to Dominic hadn't completely opened the floodgates, but they were significantly weakened.

He went into the kitchen, flicking on the radio to hear Classic FM blaring out the theme to *Pirates of the Caribbean*. Had his mate Derek been to see that and had it made him think of running round the garden shouting, "Avast!"? What had Mum said about them? *Pretending to be brave.* That's what he needed to do now: pretend to be brave, ring Eddie, and get the whole bloody thing sorted out.

Morgan thought about taking Dutch courage, but resorting to the bottle would likely loosen his tongue. He'd just have to fucking well bite the bullet, and if things went tits up, then he'd have to deal with it.

He fetched his phone and rang. Luckily his brother answered quickly, before Morgan lost his nerve.

"Hello?" the familiar voice sounded down the line.

"Hi. It's Morgan."

"Morgan? Is Mum okay?" The panicked tones did nothing to ease the situation.

"Yes, she's fine. Doing as well as can be expected." Morgan took a deep breath. "I had a bit of inner ear trouble, but it's clearing up. How are things?" They exchanged a bit of news, both sounding slightly constrained at the fact they so rarely communicated now.

"The reason I rang—apart from getting an update," Morgan added, probably unconvincingly, "was because I'd been having a clear out in the loft. You wouldn't believe how much old rubbish is up there."

"I would. Dad was always a hoarder. Found anything valuable?"

"I wish. No. Just puzzling." Another deep breath. "An old book about that shipwreck. The one the timbers came from."

"Yep? I vaguely remember something like that."

"Do you? I have no memory of it at all, but my name's in the back."

"Yeah, I know." Eddie laughed. "I was dead jealous that you got to sign in it, not me. Time I confessed."

Morgan's head spun, nothing to do with labyrinthitis this time. "What?"

"That I hid the book among all the old programmes and things. Because you were the lucky one. I was hoping you'd get cross that it had been lost." Eddie chuckled again. "You didn't. That was the most annoying thing of all."

"I didn't get cross because I had no bloody idea it existed." He was getting angry now, though. "If I had, it would have saved a lot of angst, believe me."

"Eh?"

"Long story. Don't ask." *Don't ever ask.* "If it was such a big deal, any idea *why* I don't remember anything about it?"

"Hm." Eddie paused for a moment. "Do you remember having pneumonia?"

"Sorry? What?"

"You were flat on your back with pneumonia."

"Oh, right. I know I was ill, but I'm never sure how much of the detail I remember is entirely based on what people told me afterwards." He certainly recalled with horror one bout of coughing that had racked his body to the point where he hadn't been able to breathe. The doctor had visited, but they'd kept him at home, dosed up with antibiotics and who knew what, or so he had found out later. Although what this had to do with anything...

"That's probably why you don't remember the book. It was your favourite when you were lying in bed, helpless. You kept wanting to hear it read. When they thought you were at death's door, they let you sign it."

"Death's door? Was I that bad?"

"I doubt it, given that you didn't get dragged to hospital." Eddie sounded a touch too hearty in his reassurance. "Gran got into a state about you. Dad wanted to ban her from the house, but that made it worse. She was convinced you were popping your clogs."

"Sounds like her." Morgan's increasingly strong sense of relief fought against his natural pessimism. "Didn't Mum or Dad say anything about the book going missing?"

"Not at the time. They were too worried about you being ill. Anyway, although it was Mum's book, she hated it. It used to give her nightmares, she said."

A tingle shot up Morgan's spine. "Say that again."

"Sorry?"

"Can you say that last bit again, please. The line's bad at this end, and I didn't catch it," Morgan lied.

"Mum didn't like the book because it gave her bad dreams. About shipwrecks. She'd have burned the bloody thing if it hadn't been some kind of family heirloom."

"Right." One final question. "So, if she hated it, why did she read the thing to me? I mean, I know I was a pain in the arse, always wanting my own way, and I must have been worse if I was ill, but wouldn't she have thought it might scare me?"

"She did. And you were. A pain in the arse, I mean. It was Dad who read it to you. Mum went flipping mental at him."

"I can imagine. Thanks for filling in the blanks."

"My pleasure. Don't leave it so long before you ring the next time, okay?"

"Okay. Love to all the family." Morgan ended the call, then stared again at the little book. Surely the explanation couldn't have been this simple, that this book had been the cause of so much stress and worry?

I told you so.

Morgan could almost hear Dominic's voice speaking the words. It didn't help that it seemed the bloke had been right all along.

How easy would it be to pick up the phone and put things straight? Too easy, maybe, or did he want the bloke to ask him for forgiveness?

You're the one who stopped me saying sorry all the time.

Yeah. And Morgan was the one who'd implied he didn't want a snivelling wretch for a boyfriend, like he didn't want a lying rat. Maybe he should take a whole tin of man up, get on the phone to Dominic, and plead with *him* to be forgiven, given that Morgan was the one who'd acted like a pillock time and again. If his mother had been hale, hearty, and here, she'd have stood over him, forcing him to make the call, but she wasn't there and he was too weary to make any more calls tonight. He'd sleep on it and make up his mind in the morning, because surely he'd regret acting impulsively? Only hadn't he been acting impulsively when he'd had the row with Dominic, if not this whole month?

He picked the phone up, found Dominic's number, and pressed Call.

After what seemed an age—long enough for Morgan to think Dominic had seen the name of the incoming caller and was ignoring him—the call connected.

"Hello?" Dominic's tone was cool.

"Hi, it's me." Morgan felt tongue-tied, unsure of where to start. After being so adamant that he wanted rid of Dominic, he now regretted not having the bloke in the room with him. It was hard enough talking over the phone, but when it was something as tricky as this, both parties needed to see the facial expressions accompanying the words.

"I guessed that." Dominic went silent; he clearly wasn't going to make this easy, but why should he?

"I've got some news."

"Right." His tone was more conciliatory now. "Have you seen the doctor?"

"Appointment's not yet, remember? I'm not cancelling it," Morgan added hastily, not wanting to risk an argument. "Are you still in Cornwall?"

"Yeah. Been doing a bit of walking, up on the headland, where Lawson's supposed to have been killed. Only I suppose you're not that interested now."

"I am. Got some news about him too. Some old stuff of my dad's I found in the attic. I'd forgotten all about the research he'd done, which made me get in a state, of course." Morgan shook his head; this was too hard. "I'm not making much sense. Can we meet up?"

"I'll come round."

"You don't need to. I mean, I'd like it if you did, but I feel guilty calling you over here every two minutes."

"You feel guilty about everything." Dominic produced half a chuckle.

"I know I do. I have to grow a pair sometime."

"As I remember, you have a magnificent pair already." The half chuckle had developed into a full blown—and extremely lascivious—laugh.

"Stop it." Morgan couldn't help but grin.

"Get the coffee maker on. I'll be twenty minutes. Longer if the grockles are out in force."

"I'll get the biscuits out too." Those bloody biscuits—they'd been as integral to his relationship with Dominic as the ship or the sex. And the way his stomach had started to churn, he wasn't convinced he could keep even a digestive down.

While the coffee brewed, Morgan took all the stuff from the loft through into the dining room. It was easier to spread the material out there, and less of a temptation to spread himself out on the settee and hint he and Dominic use sex to solve their communication problems. It would be a pretty effective solution if a cowardly one, and would just put off the moment he and Dominic had to talk things through. He tried to arrange it neatly, but found himself all fingers and thumbs so left it strewn.

By the time Morgan heard the car crunch up the gravel drive, he'd worked himself into a bit of a state, nearly dropping the entire plate of biscuits and having to wipe crumbs off the family trees. When Morgan opened the door to let his guest in, Dominic looked in as much of a lather, tension in his brow and dark-rimmed eyes suggesting a lack of sleep.

"Are you all right?"

Dominic frowned. "I'm supposed to be asking you that. How's the head?"

"Fine." Morgan ushered him in. "Actually, I had a bit of a dizzy spell earlier, but it really is getting better. Honest." It was time he started being frank.

"Good. Just don't cancel your doctor's appointment."

"I won't." Morgan got Dominic settled in the dining room, letting him go through the papers—all bar the note and the book—while he fetched the mugs of coffee. He stood at the dining room door, watching with pleasure Dominic's intense concentration, before asking, "What do you think?"

"Interesting stuff." Dominic glanced up, delight on his face. He took his drink. "Thanks."

"No worries. You can keep the book with the history of the church, by the way." Morgan cradled his mug, tension gradually ebbing from his shoulders.

"Can I? Double thanks, then." Dominic smoothed over the book's cover with those long, expressive fingers. "Was all this up in your loft?"

"Yep. Right treasure trove up there. I'd forgotten all about it."

Dominic glanced over again, smiling. "Realising that would have given you a fright, I guess."

"It did, especially coming on the heels of visiting Mum."

Dominic paled. "Has anything happened?"

"No. She's as well as she could be, physically; she got herself a bit upset." Morgan explained what had happened during his visit, what Christine had told him about the dreams recurring across the generations. "It was the last thing I wanted to hear. By the time I went rummaging for these, I was convinced I was on the slippery slope to premature senility."

Dominic stretched his arm out, as though to touch Morgan's hand, then quickly withdrew it. "You must have been through hell."

"I have. And it's made me appreciate the fact I'm a total idiot." Morgan picked up a biscuit, rolling it between his fingers but not eating it. "I should have got a doctor to check the contents of my head ages ago."

"Would he or she have found anything in there?" Dominic smiled. "I know I'm not allowed to say sorry, but I'm saying it. I've been too eager to tell you your fears were stupid, that there was a rational explanation, rather than listen and focus on giving you a bit of comfort. I'm glad you're getting some professional help. Not because I think you *are* going loopy, but to help you see things in perspective. Stop you getting stressed."

"You're forgiven for the apology. And it's returned too, because it turns out I might have been fretting over nothing, like you said." Morgan slipped his hand onto the chair next to his, where he'd hidden the note and book, bringing them out to lay on the table. "Have a read of this." He pushed the story of the shipwreck across to Dominic, then made an attempt on the biscuit. He'd thought he wouldn't be able to manage eating it, but his appetite had returned with a vengeance, and he'd polished off a handful of them by the time Dominic had reached the end of the tale.

"This reads like a script for your nightmare," Dominic said, looking up from the text at last.

"Seems like it. Mum's nightmare, too, if Christine's to be believed. Have a gander at the final page."

Dominic turned to the list of names, then whistled. "Bloody hell. Did you know about this?"

"Of course I didn't." Morgan related the phone conversation with Eddie, while Dominic listened, nodding his head as the story unfolded. "Seems like there was one bit of family history I was oblivious of. The key bit as probably turns out."

"It would certainly explain a lot. Especially if your subconscious associates the story of the wreck with the time when you were so ill. No wonder it gives you the creeps." Dominic raised his hand. "Sorry. Getting into the pseudo-psychology again. I need to learn to give it a miss."

"You do, if you don't want to risk being a pain in the arse."

"Takes one to know one." Dominic shook his head. "I really like you. I can't help being an old-fashioned pompous prick, and it's too late to do anything about that fact, but I'm trying my best."

"I know you are. I'd not have asked you back if I hadn't thought you were tolerable. I could have posted all this lot." Morgan studied his dad's little note in his hands; it might have been the plum piece of information, but he wasn't ready to share it yet. "It might have been easier if there hadn't been so much stuff going on. Mum. Me feeling sorry for myself over James. Me feeling sorry for you because I'd made you stay over that first bank holiday. That bloody attack of labyrinthitis. Me getting myself shit scared and not wanting you to see what a state I was getting into. Not wanting you to suffer what I'd suffered with Mum."

"Is that why you told me to piss off?" Dominic didn't seem cross, just bemused.

"Yes. I mean I don't think I thought it through quite that rationally—I was too frightened to think of anything logically—but that's what it came down to. It's no fun watching somebody you're close to lose it."

Dominic nodded slowly, clearly choosing his words with care. "You don't need to say yes, but if it would help to have somebody around for a bit, while you see the doctor and get yourself sorted out, I'd be available. The woman from the HR department has been nagging me to book the time off I carried over from last year, and these few days haven't eaten it all up."

"I didn't realise you were such a workaholic."

"I'm not. Sad thing is, I had no real incentive to take a break before."

Morgan felt torn again. If he agreed to Dominic's plan, would it be for the right motive? Did he want Dominic here for his own sake?

"Is it that hard a decision?" Dominic was evidently trying to sound jokey, but the concern in his voice couldn't be hidden.

"Only for a fucking idiot like me." Morgan took Dominic's hand. "I'd really like you to stay for a few extra days, if you could. After that, we'll take it as it comes. Not create problems if we don't have to."

"That works for me." Mingled relief and delight illuminated Dominic's face. "I'll get on the phone to them tomorrow. I can always work remotely if there's anything urgent to deal with." He squeezed Morgan's hand. "I'm pleased you trust me. I do know what a big thing it was for you to tell me about that nightmare, and I guess it's even bigger getting me alongside now. I mean, not that I think you're going gaga, but—"

"Oh, shut up." Morgan pushed back his chair, rounded the table, and plonked his backside on the edge of it, leaning down to give Dominic a kiss. Not a full-blooded passionate lip-smacker, but one that could be a promise of things to come if both parties agreed.

"Not sure either of us deserve that, but thanks." Dominic beamed.

"I've got something else for you too. Not that!" Morgan sniggered as he caught Dominic eyeing up his crotch. "Not at the moment, anyway. And you might like this more."

"How could I like anything more than having it away with you?"

"Reserve judgement on that until you've seen it." Morgan produced his dad's note, like a conjuror.

Dominic read it, whistled, read it a second time, then gave Morgan a cautious smile. "This *is* genuine, isn't it? You didn't fake it to keep me happy?"

"Don't overvalue yourself." Morgan slapped his arm. "Of course it's real. That's Dad's writing. And before you ask, I haven't seen anything else about the medallion, although you're welcome to take your chances with the spiders up in the loft and turn everything out a second time."

"I might take you up on that." Dominic read the note again. "Seems like this story's going to run and run."

"Don't get too excited. It might still be a wild-goose chase."

"It might. But I don't care." Dominic got out of his chair and wrapped his arms round Morgan's waist. "Remember I said I'd always wanted to live round here? I've kept an eye out for jobs in the area, and there's a firm in Launceston that's got a vacancy recently come up. Closing date end of June. I don't know whether I should apply."

"Of course you should. What the fuck's stopping you?"

"I didn't want to risk bumping into you." He held Morgan tighter. "If you were still not talking to me, and if I'd got the job and moved here, I'd have looked like one of those weird blokes who stalk their ex."

"Daft bugger." They shared a kiss—a rougher, deeper, longer kiss than the previous one, the memory of what they'd done before acting itself out in the way their bodies moved together. The snug fit of flesh on flesh both comfortable and stimulating. "Steady on," Morgan gasped, at last. "Dining room table's too hard to do it on."

"You've tried, have you?" Dominic pressed closer. "Shame. It would feel good, doing it under these beams, given that they brought us together."

Morgan laughed. "I should have known you only wanted me for my carpenters' marks."

"You've got some of those on you too? I never noticed. Still, I guess it was dark."

"We could leave the light on. This time."

"We could." Dominic pulled Morgan off the table and into his arms. "We will."

On reaching the bedroom door, Dominic halted, his expression momentarily guarded.

Morgan took his arm. "What's wrong?"

"Just checking this is what you want. Speak now or forever hold your peace and all that."

"My peace is not what I want to hold. Your piece, however . . ."

Dominic grinned, clearly relieved. "I thought I was supposed to be inspecting *you*?"

"There's time for both." Morgan edged them through the door and into his room. The bed was still a mess from the morning, but neither of them was worried about that, both in too much of a hurry to get their clothes off and search for those imaginary marks. Dominic alleged he'd spotted some on Morgan's back, in the very place he could never check without ricking his neck. Which meant he'd have to check over the rest of Morgan's body to see if any others had eluded him—which he did, inch by inch, with fingers and lips, unable to resist making the odd smutty nautical joke while he was at it. Most of which seemed to concern masts.

Morgan went along with everything, amused to have at last found somebody who saw the funny side of sex. Well, wasn't it a faintly ludicrous business?

And when they eventually climaxed, in a tangled heap on the tangled bed, it felt like coming home; a sailor back from sea finding himself in a safe and familiar haven.

Sometime in the middle of the night, Morgan stirred from a peaceful, dreamless sleep. He reached for a drink of water, and noticed Dominic lying awake, watching him by the moonlight streaming in through the window.

"You okay?"

"Never been better." Dominic rubbed his tousled head against Morgan's. "Counting my blessings. Among which is you not having a nightmare tonight."

"I've not had one in ages." Morgan remembered counting his own blessings—albeit finding them few and flimsy—when he'd had the Dear John letter. How things had changed. He snuggled back down, but the moon's brightness disturbed him. Reluctantly, he eased out of the embrace. "I should shut those curtains, or I won't get back to sleep."

"You stay there and rest. Let me."

Morgan watched as Dominic slipped out of bed and—body silvered in the moonlight—moved across to the window.

"Don't shut them just yet. That light suits you." Morgan left the bed to join his love, slipping an arm round Dominic's wiry frame and resting against his shoulder.

"That's nice. Here, listen. We've got background music."

Owls were hooting out in the silver birches, whose branches gently rustled in the breeze. A summer night's symphony, or an overture to romance. Morgan thought he could detect a suspiration of the waves—or was that simply his imagination?

"It's magical," he said, leaning closer into a hug which was turning distinctly amorous again. "I don't mean any of that superstitious nonsense. The magic of the real world and all its wonders."

"Is real love magic, as well?" Dominic whispered against his neck.

"Something like that, maybe." Morgan had thought he loved James and that James loved him, but now he wasn't so sure. There'd never really been a sense of "for better or worse" with the Rat. Not like he'd found with Dominic. "Not yet."

"There's still hope, then." Dominic nuzzled against Morgan's neck. "I've been trying hard not to, but there's every chance I'll fall in love with you. As I've been allowed to say sorry today, I'll apologise for it in advance."

"You're such a drip." Morgan chuckled. "I'm too tired and confused to know where my heart's at, but I do know this feels different to how it was with James. Less like a brand-new suit than a comfy old jumper."

"And you're such a romantic. Not." Dominic kissed him. "Coming here feels like coming home."

Maybe one day it would be. But that was a conversation for another time. In the meanwhile, it was getting nippy and there was a big, warm, comfy bed to hand. Morgan edged them towards it.

"What about the curtains?" Dominic whispered.

"Sod them. I'll use the moonlight to search for your carpenters' marks. All over. Mast and all."

Explore more of the *Porthkennack* universe:
riptidepublishing.com/titles/universe/porthkennack

a PORTHKENNACK CONTEMPORARY

Wake Up Call
JL Merrow

House of Cards
Garrett Leigh

Foxglove Copse
Alex Beecroft

Junkyard Heart
Garrett Leigh

a PORTHKENNACK HISTORICAL

Count the Shells
Charlie Cochrane

A Gathering Storm
Joanna Chambers

Dear Reader,

Thank you for reading Charlie Cochrane's *Broke Deep*!

We know your time is precious and you have many, many entertainment options, so it means a lot that you've chosen to spend your time reading. We really hope you enjoyed it.

We'd be honored if you'd consider posting a review—good or bad—on sites like **Amazon, Barnes & Noble, Kobo, Goodreads, Twitter, Facebook, Tumblr,** and your blog or website. We'd also be honored if you told your friends and family about this book. Word of mouth is a book's lifeblood!

For more information on upcoming releases, author interviews, blog tours, contests, giveaways, and more, please sign up for our weekly, spam-free newsletter and visit us around the web:

Newsletter: tinyurl.com/RiptideSignup
Twitter: twitter.com/RiptideBooks
Facebook: facebook.com/RiptidePublishing
Goodreads: tinyurl.com/RiptideOnGoodreads
Tumblr: riptidepublishing.tumblr.com

Thank you so much for Reading the Rainbow!

RiptidePublishing.com

ACKNOWLEDGEMENTS

Thanks to all the Porthkennack team—authors Alex Beecroft, JL Merrow, Joanna Chambers, and Garrett Leigh, and editors Sarah Lyons and Caz Galloway—for helping to make this happen.

ALSO BY
CHARLIE COCHRANE

Best Corpse for the Job
Jury of One
Count the Shells (coming soon)

Lessons for Survivors
Lessons for Suspicious Minds
Lessons for Idle Tongues
Lessons for Sleeping Dogs

Coming Soon
Lessons in Love
Lessons in Desire
Lessons in Discovery
Lessons in Power
Lessons in Temptation
Lessons in Seduction
Lessons in Trust
All Lessons Learned

Paired Novellas
Wild Bells
Home Fires Burning
In the Spotlight

Novellas and Short Stories
Second Helpings
Awfully Glad
Don't Kiss the Vicar
Promises Made Under Fire
Tumble Turn
Dreams of a Hero
Wolves of the West
Music in the Midst of
Desolation

Anthologies (contributing author)
Pride of Poppies
Capital Crimes
Lashings of Sauce
Tea and Crumpet
British Flash
Summer's Day

ABOUT
THE AUTHOR

Because Charlie Cochrane couldn't be trusted to do any of her jobs of choice—like managing a rugby team—she writes. Her mystery novels include the Edwardian era Cambridge Fellows series, and the contemporary Lindenshaw Mysteries.

A member of the Romantic Novelists' Association, Mystery People and International Thriller Writers Inc, Charlie regularly appears at literary festivals and at reader and author conferences with The Deadly Dames.

Where to find her:
Website: charliecochrane.wordpress.com
Facebook: facebook.com/charlie.cochrane.18
Twitter: twitter.com/charliecochrane
Goodreads:
goodreads.com/author/show/2727135.Charlie_Cochrane

Enjoy more stories like
Broke Deep
at RiptidePublishing.com!

Home the Hard Way
ISBN: 978-1-62649-146-5

The Secret of Hunter's Bog
ISBN: 978-1-62649-374-2

Earn Bonus Bucks!
Earn 1 Bonus Buck for each dollar you spend. Find out how at
RiptidePublishing.com/news/bonus-bucks.

Win Free Ebooks for a Year!
Pre-order coming soon titles directly through our site and you'll
receive one entry into a drawing for a chance to win free books for
a year! Get the details at RiptidePublishing.com/contests.